# End of the Trail

One short week ago, Malcolm had the town in the palm of his hand. Now a bartender laughed in his face and a sheepherder snickered behind his back.

He'd been sure that his past lay safely buried, that no one would ever know about the way he had lied and cheated and murdered . . .

Then the Texan came to town, a stranger he had never met yet who knew all about him . . . a stranger who was twisting his past into a hangman's noose and winding it tightly about his neck.

He would have to stop him. There was no other choice.

## Other SIGNET Westerns
## You Will Want to Read

☐ **HIGH VENGEANCE by Frank O'Rourke.** The time for vengeance had come and Bryan plans to kill the woman who had destroyed his father.
(#P4000—60¢)

☐ **ACTION AT THREE PEAKS by Frank O'Rourke.** An action-packed story about a soldier who leads a charge against the Indians, only to return to the fort to face the woman he had once loved.
(#P4079—60¢)

☐ **VIOLENT COUNTRY by Frank O'Rourke.** Set in the exciting West, a young man sets out after the Cochise, and will be successful unless the girl he loves gets to him first. (#P3873—60¢)

☐ **WEB OF GUNSMOKE by Will Hickok.** Several men behind a gun can only spell trouble—and there's plenty of it in this exciting western.
(#P4139—60¢)

☐ **TRAIL TO TUCSON by Ray Hogan.** A loner takes on more than he bargains for when he vows to protect a woman and the $20,000 in her saddlebag. (#P4031—60¢)

---

**THE NEW AMERICAN LIBRARY, INC., P.O. Box 2310, Grand Central Station, New York, New York 10017**

Please send me the SIGNET BOOKS I have checked above. I am enclosing $_____(check or money order—no currency or C.O.D.'s). Please include the list price plus 10¢ a copy to cover mailing costs. (New York City residents add 6% Sales Tax. Other New York State residents add 3% plus any local sales or use taxes.)

Name_____

Address_____

City_____State_____Zip Code_____

Allow at least 3 weeks for delivery

★
★ ★
★

# A
# TEXAN
# CAME
# RIDING

*FRANK O'ROURKE*

★
★ ★
★ ★
★ ★
★ ★
★ ★
★

A SIGNET BOOK from
**NEW AMERICAN LIBRARY**
TIMES MIRROR

© 1958 BY FRANK O'ROURKE

*All rights reserved*

FOURTH PRINTING

SIGNET TRADEMARK REG. U.S. PAT. OFF. AND FOREIGN COUNTRIES
REGISTERED TRADEMARK—MARCA REGISTRADA
HECHO EN CHICAGO, U.S.A.

SIGNET, SIGNET CLASSICS, MENTOR AND PLUME BOOKS
*are published by The New American Library, Inc.,
1301 Avenue of the Americas, New York, New York 10019*

FIRST PRINTING, JUNE, 1958

PRINTED IN THE UNITED STATES OF AMERICA

# Chapter One

THE fresh smell of mint was in the air. Kearney had crushed some between his fingers as he rose from drinking, and he lingered in the juniper shade with lemon sunlight filtering through the branches across his face, remembering other years when fresh, bright smells brought a surge of fresh joy to life. What was it about mint, and mown hay, honey and apples and spice, that made happiness grow stronger? Was it the simple joy of living fully, or the senses reacting with typical human greed to rich smells? He did not know and he could never make the spent pilgrimage again; youth's fine-honed edge of enjoyment was dulled beyond full repair. He smelled the mint, holding his fingers to his nose, and turned from the river to the waiting stage.

"Hurry up!" the driver called. "Late now."

Kearney took his seat and rode the bucking stage up the side canyon trail from the river gorge onto the plateau, eight racking, dusty miles until they trotted on hard-baked adobe earth between the low houses into the plaza of Taos where the courthouse dominated the scene, lying brown and aged against the brown earth, looking out upon the ancient town from barred, glassless windows and casing-sprung doors, an old building whose roots thrust undying and forever watered by two hundred years of mountains and valley and river running to the sea. Kearney smelled his mint-stained fingers, shutting off the odor of manure and urine and earth, all trod and packed through the centuries by too many conflicting races of men.

"Taos," the driver said. "You go to the hotel, mister?"

"Yes," Kearney said. "But later."

He carried his scarred Gladstone into the courthouse toward the door sign marking the sheriff's office, and began it then, knowing before he inquired about Malcolm that he was triggering a sequence of events as certain in their future unfolding as sunrise and death. He needed Poe's black raven riding his shoulder to truly foretell the trouble he might bring.

"Sheriff Montez?" he said.

"Yes."

"My name is John Kearney. Are you busy now?"

Adolfo Montez rose from his chair and closed the door. He was lean and gray and daintily light on his small feet; and turning, offering his hand and a gold-toothed smile, he fitted perfectly the description given Kearney in Santa Fe, capital of New Mexico, seventy miles to the south: quick-witted, occupying a difficult position, heir by blood and custom to the weaknesses of his time and kind. Take a bribe, yes, but pursue and hang a guilty man with that same smile. Outwardly indolent, sharp and perceptive within. Worth knowing well, worth treating with courtesy and respect.

"Now," Adolfo Montez said briskly. "How may I help you, Mr. Kearney?"

"Read these," Kearney said. He passed the letters, stood silent while the sheriff read, then held the tintype beneath the windowlight. "Do you know this man?"

Adolfo Montez studied the tintype a full minute. "A mustache, thinner, but those eyes—the eagle's eyes! Yes, it could be Mr. Malcolm. But I do not understand. Is he wanted?"

"You've read the letters?"

"Yes, and very fine ones too, asking me to help you in any way possible. But you are not an officer of the law, Mr. Kearney. What then do you want?"

"What the letters say."

"Yes, yes," Montez said. "But this help—will it be legal, under the jurisdiction of my office?"

"I don't know," Kearney said.

"You confuse me," Montez said. "But call on me at any time."

"You can start now," Kearney said. "Tell me all you know about Charles Malcolm."

He pushed the Gladstone aside, took a chair, and waited. He watched Montez respond to his deliberately blunt question with a bland facial gyration that drew veils across the sharp brown eyes.

"Malcolm has lived here six years," Montez said. "He practices law, he owns land, a mine, he is very wealthy. He comes from England but he speaks the best Spanish, he is well known in the community. What else can I say, Mr. Kearney?"

"Well known?" Kearney asked.

"Oh yes."

"You do not say well liked?"

"We all have our likes and dislikes," Montez said. "I may admire a man, others may detest him. You see?"

"I see," Kearney said. "Many thanks."

He paused at the door, facing the dark, odorous hallway, and glanced back at the sheriff.

"No need for secrecy," he said. "If you happen to be one of those men who admire Malcolm, you can tell him."

"I gave no opinion," Montez said gently. "I only expressed the sentiment of the town."

"You've been sheriff eleven years," Kearney said.

"Yes."

"I know how you did it," Kearney said. "I'd guess you'll hold it down another eleven. Thank you again. I'll be at the hotel from now on."

He left the courthouse and threaded his way across the plaza to the Columbian Hotel on the southwest corner. He took the best room, upstairs in front, a big dusty room with one window, solid plank floor and door, and a huge old bed that sagged dangerously beneath the weight of faded army blankets, plus the undeniable fact that the springs were beyond redemption. Kearney opened his bag and set out his change of clothing, his shaving gear, his holster and cloth-wrapped revolver. He had no strict orders, he would follow no set routine. He could approach Malcolm as he saw fit, go directly to the man or wait until Malcolm heard the news and came to him. Riding up from Santa Fe on the narrow gauge to Taos Junction, transferring to the stage and making the long, rough ride, he had given the problem little thought. He would now, in the hour before sunset while he washed, changed clothes, and went downstairs for a drink. That was time enough to digest his first impressions of the town. Kearney trusted his feel of a town as it came to him in those early minutes; he had found it wisest, in the past, to reach a decision and follow it through. That way he started something; it might be wrong, but the tide of human nature had a way of washing everything onto the shore. He had traveled eight hundred miles into a strange land; now let it begin.

There was an inner room behind the sheriff's office and the connecting door was always ajar. That room was used for arms and ammunition, for the questioning of unruly prisoners, for loafing purposes by deputies. Carlos Ramos had sat quietly in that dark little room while the stranger talked with Montez; after the sheriff left for supper Ramos departed by the back door, took the alley to Pueblo Road, and walked one block north to a high adobe wall hiding the big house from the road. He went through the gate and up the path beneath the cottonwoods to the deep-set front door, knocked sharply three times, and waited in the shadows. He heard the big dog sniffing inside, growling deep in that great hairy chest, then padding aside as the Judas window opened.

"Well, Ramos," Charles Malcolm said. "What do you want?"

"A man just came to the sheriff," Ramos said. "Listen..."

When Ramos finished his version of the conversation, the face withdrew, returned, and one eye regarded Ramos coldly.

"Thank you. Vigil will see you tonight."

"Thank *you*," Ramos said. "I——"

The window snapped shut and he stood alone, words tumbling on his tongue, forever frustrated by such a man. Then he grinned philosophically and ambled down the path. What did it matter? The Indian would pay him tonight and he'd drink to Malcolm—but only his first drink. Subsequent glasses of brandy were dedicated to simple thoughts and uncomplicated pleasures.

Malcolm said, "Come, Oso," and led the big dog down the long center hall to the back room. He passed empty rooms, dusty and unused, but the back room was furnished in a manner alien to the adobe walls and vigas and dirt floor. The furniture was hand-carved, native in origin, but each chest and table formed a platform for those mysterious objects so dear to the town's gossipy ears: the silver set with the gadroon borders, the Haviland china, the rugs and vases, the pictures in their polished silver frames. The house was composed of nine rooms, but here was the center of Malcolm's life within those walls, and here he stood beside the great table that served as desk and called into the patio and waited until the Indian appeared.

"Give Ramos five dollars tonight," Malcolm said. "And take this card to a man at the hotel. His name is John Kearney."

Vigil took the silver dollars, then, after Malcolm wrote and blotted, the white card with the brief message. Vigil nodded silently, the faintest smile wisp touching his mouth, brushing thin wrinkles across his flat cheeks to the lobes of his close-set ears. He padded away into the house depths and Malcolm smiled, watching him go, for he understood the Indian's feeling toward all deputies. Vigil found satanic humor in knowing that Ramos could be bought for five silver dollars, while he was valued much higher. Ramos sneered at Vigil, and Vigil took his revenge in the silent Indian way. Malcolm smiled at his desk, hands building a thought steeple, mind absorbed in the sudden appearance of John Kearney.

In momentary repose Malcolm was not the typical remittance man with thin mustache and iron gray hair, Oxford accent, impeccable manners, and overbearing way. Here was a man whose antecedents were buried in the past, a man of forty-five who had crowded an intolerable amount of life into that time, so that he forever gave others the feeling he had never been a child, even a young man, but had sprung full grown from the womb, fitted completely with all the cunning charm and roguery of the thorough scoundrel.

He was a tall man when first measured by eye. Only when sized against tall men did his height show him a mere average mortal of five-eight. It was the man himself who stood tall in other eyes, the force and power in him, his bearing and walk and manner. His hair was jet black and lay smooth over his round skull, trimmed neatly above tiny ears and parted on the left. He was cleanshaven, his nose long and thin, his gray eyes set wide beneath a high forehead, his mouth very wide and flexible, curling into the smooth, cynical leanness of his cheeks so that all his emotions were masked, subtle to capture and never entirely understood.

His shoulders sloped womanlike into long arms and clean, graceful hands. His legs were pipestems but encased had a look of strength and agility denied by the skinny calves and whipstring thighs. He wore black boots and gray trousers, white shirts, black string ties and, on occasion, cravats; and he boasted a variety of coats that caused one young padre to call him Beau Brummel. He wore an old hunting coat habitually, brown tweed, patched and darned at the elbows, belted in back and faced with narrow lapels. Wearing that coat, with the broad-brimmed black Stetson he adopted upon arrival in Taos, astride a good horse, he was a striking figure. He was only an average horseman, for he had not earned his seat the usual way—on the hurricane deck of a hundred broncs. His other coats were black and gray and brown, brown for casual wear, gray for mornings, the black for court days and calls in homes around the valley where formality cut such a deep, lasting impression in the old Spanish pride and custom.

He knew when to talk and when to listen. For the most part he made his wants and desires known swiftly, and wasted not a word thereafter. He would disappear for days on end into the mountains, turn morose and sullen at odd times, drink like a fish in his own house, yet he was a charming host and his prowess with the ladies had become a legend in a country where such prowess was the status quo. He had fathered a number of bastards, which only proved his manhood and did not lessen his stature, he charmed old men and ladies, he had a way with young men and children, he was all things to all people; yet within him lay a negation, a rareness of feeling that betrayed him in his complete indifference to his bastards, a denial of the warm, dark beauty he took so freely and refused with equal freeness once that beauty was marred by the fat of childbirth. He pleased only his own body, he loaned himself briefly and gave nothing in return. For he had no love in him, he could offer no true warmth to anyone. He trusted no one but Vigil, the Indian. No one else.

He sat at his desk and thought of John Kearney, and the worry was a small, spreading ripple in his mind. Six years without worry, now it came again from the past. He had fled from his past all of his life, and here, for six years, he had believed himself safely lost forever. The irony of Kearney's arrival was not discovery; it was wonder over which segment of that past had brought the man. Malcolm honestly did not know. He doubted that Gabriel, on the Judgment Day, could untangle his past and brand him with the worst of many sins.

Kearney listened to the bartender, a tall man named Wintergreen, talk wool prices and weather with a stooped little fellow named Shaffer, neither interested in the other's words, simply worrying the familiar old bones of contention in a lazy, whisky-flavored fashion.

Three half-drunk cowboys played cooncan in the far corner, and a crippled man with a broom lingered in the shadows, dabbing the floor and cocking his poor, foolish head at the sage words of his betters. Into that atmosphere Kearney first heard the moccasin shuffle, then saw the Indian materialize beside him and place the white card at his elbow.

"Kearney?" the Indian asked.

"Yes."

"For you."

He read the note: "Would you honor me with a visit at your convenience this evening? Charles Malcolm."

"When?" the Indian said.

"I'm having a drink," Kearney said. "Then supper. Then I'm going to bed. If Malcolm wants to see me, I'll be around here."

"You won't come?"

"No," he said. "Are you looking for an argument?"

"All right," the Indian said. "I'll tell him."

The Indian had measured him and that description was returning posthaste to Malcolm, complete to the last detail.

As the Indian turned away Kearney said, "Hold on," and lifted one boot to knee level. "Just in case you missed the brand," he said. "Fourteen-inch top, Heyer-made . . . and I'm wearing socks."

"Thank you, señor," the Indian said indifferently, and disappeared through the street door, leaving Kearney with a smile at his own defeat, for the Indian had won that round hands down. He motioned to the bartender and said, "Who was that?"

"Vigil," Wintergreen said. "He's Malcolm's man Friday. Was he bothering you?"

"Mistaken identity," Kearney said.

"Another round?"

"No thanks," he said. "Time for supper."

He passed through the lobby into the dining room, took a corner table facing the street, and settled himself for the meal. It had broken with unexpected swiftness and left him doubting the sheriff. He had judged

Montez a man who did not sell out cheap; but someone had passed the news within thirty minutes.

"No peppers," he told the girl. "Just beans and steak, plenty of tortillas."

"And coffee, señor?"

"Yes," he said. "Keep it filled till I yell uncle."

"Uncle?" she said. "Tio?"

"Nothing," Kearney smiled. "Just a saying from my country."

He ate, watching dusk melt and thicken into blue night, saw windows across the plaza pop into squares of yellow. Shaffer, the stooped little sheepman, trailed his delicate aroma into the dining room and hunched over a front table; others came and ate; Wintergreen was busy in the barroom, his thin, nasal voice rising above that throaty hum. All the life of the valley placed impressions here in the plaza: the wagons in from ranches and sheep camps for six months' supplies of groceries and hardware; the miners down from the hills; the people of the valley who farmed the tiny slatlike sections of *vega* land and pasture along the creeks; even an artist he had seen crossing from the courthouse, a small and wiry little man carrying a sketch pad and talking vociferously with a big man in boots and khaki pants; it was all here in the plaza, or it came during the days and nights. Kearney was stretching his fifth cup of coffee when the man entered, glanced at him across the room, and came directly down the center aisle. Charles Malcolm bent his head in a curt gesture and did not remove his hat.

"Mr. Kearney?"

"Yes."

Malcolm said, "Nothing, leave us," and sent the girl scurrying away toward the kitchen. Kearney felt the silence around them as dinnerware stopped biting plates and heads were lifted slyly, a short silence that followed Malcolm's entrance and broke reluctantly into discordant speech.

"Very rude of you, Mr. Kearney," Malcolm said. "Refusing my cordial invitation."

"It got results," Kearney said.

"Curious, you see," Malcolm said. "I'm a great lover of nature. Make a study of flora and fauna."

"You meant insects," Kearney said. "Put your specimen pin in your case, Malcolm. I don't stick easy. What's bothering you?"

"You misunderstand," Malcolm said.

"Your grapevine works fast," Kearney said. "How do you pay off, once a month or by the piece?"

"Please, Mr. Kearney," Malcolm said curtly. "Don't be crude. Tongues in trees, let us say, books in the running brooks, sermons in stones—but then, you wouldn't understand."

"No?" Kearney said. "I understand that you're no duke."

He drew blood there, for Malcolm frowned and seemed to draw himself inward. "You surprise me, Mr. Kearney. You know the quotation."

"Sure," he said. "Courtesy of Bull Durham. It won't fit out here anyway. I'm here to see you, you got the word, do you want to talk business now or let it simmer?"

"What sort of business, Mr. Kearney?"

"Sit down," he said.

"Will it take that long?" Malcolm said wearily. "Very well."

Malcolm took the chair across the table and made no move toward his hat. Kearney reached below the table on the adjoining chair and lifted his hat. He placed it squarely on his head, gave it a tap, and sat back from the table. He scored once more, watching color rise in Malcolm's face as they faced each other with the black Stetson and the flat-topped brown hat placing their faces in shadow.

"Well, Mr. Kearney?" Malcolm said softly. "Begin your tale."

"I'll make it brief," he said.

"Please do," Malcolm said. "I find myself wasting entirely too much time on drifters."

"I'm a drifter from the Big Bend country," Kearney said. "Been down there ten years. Before that I lived a while near Madison, Nebraska. You stopped there eight years ago. You knew my father's sister and her husband. Easy name to remember . . . Jones. You also knew their daughter. No use going into detail over how they finally tracked you down up here. Sort of a grab bag deal. Seems like they bumped into some other folks from New York and Illinois and Kansas all hunting you. One thing led to another, and here I am. I feel like a corporation lawyer. I've got so many claims to present I don't know where to start. But let's begin with my uncle. You can't repay one thing you owe him, Malcolm, so that leaves the least important. You owe him nine thousand dollars and forget the interest. Do you want to pay me in cash or check?"

He had deliberately spoken to the point; now he lit a cigar and waited for the explosion. Malcolm had sat expressionless while he talked, and Malcolm laughed softly and brought one hand upward in a gesture of approval.

"Mr. Kearney," Malcolm said. "You beat anything I've ever seen or heard . . . and you understand, that takes in considerable territory. I could sit here and play dumb, but you've been painfully honest with me. Assuming all this is true, where is proof of my debt to this gentleman from Nebraska? To these other good people from distant parts? Show me some proof, Mr. Kearney, and I'll concede you a weak case in law. A mortgage, a note, an IOU, anything. Please, where is your proof?"

"No papers," Kearney said. "You know that. You left nothing but trouble behind you."

"So it is their word against mine," Malcolm said. "That's scarcely proof of an honest debt."

"Their word," Kearney said. "Their tears and grief, their honest word. That's good enough for me. You're my man. I know it, you know it, let's waste no time . . . are you paying up?"

He had expected denial and Malcolm surprised him. He saw the long fingers rest on the table with no nervousness, saw the face, still smiling, voice no protest. One hand lifted again, a gesture of patience.

"Come now," Malcolm said pleasantly. "You owe me more than the bare bones, Mr. Kearney. I'm admitting nothing, but assuming this is true, how did you find me?"

"I didn't," Kearney said. "They all did, Malcolm. They hired the best and it took even them about eight years. Just following a trail, you know, like a skunk's. The smell hangs on a long time."

"You have a quick tongue, Mr. Kearney."

"Who volunteers to slow it down?" he said.

"And if I say nay?" Malcolm said. "What then, Mr. Kearney? You have given your position away. I assume you refer to the Pinkertons. Say they found me. You are not a law officer. That means one thing to a lawyer—they had no legal case. Your long journey in vain, no case in law, eh. What then, Mr. Kearney?"

"That's why I took the job," Kearney said. "Then I start."

"Start what, Mr. Kearney?"

"On you," he said. "I'll give you a day. This time tomorrow night to pay my uncle's claim. After that we'll go into the others. Pay up or I'll start."

"You bore me," Malcolm said softly. "Start what?"

"To get you," Kearney said. "Get you any way I can."

Malcolm rose suddenly and drummed his fingers on the red-and-white oilcloth. "Would you rather I paid, Mr. Kearney?"

"Why, no," Kearney said. "Now I've seen you, I'd like it better the hard way."

"Let me answer you then," Malcolm said. "I will not be here tomorrow night. I will not pay you a wooden nickel. Instead, here is my suggestion: be on your way by tomorrow night or I'll react in kind."

"Thanks," he said quietly.

"For what?"

"For getting me squared around," Kearney said. "You know how it is when you go in blind. I couldn't know till I saw you. Everything they told me, all of it, mounted up pretty high for one man. Now I know. It's all true."

"Mr. Kearney," Malcolm said coldly. "No man talks to me in that way. Don't do it again."

"I've always been a damn fool," Kearney said easily.

"So I'll just commence by calling you an overstuffed, worthless bastard. You've lied and cheated and murdered your way from wherever you started. You want me to talk a little louder, Malcolm? I'll say it again with more decorations if you don't hear so good."

He waited, drawing his feet beneath him, watching the shapeless brown tweed coat and the hands, holding himself ready; and he saw the wildness rise and boil in the gray eyes, then subside as the man caught himself up. Malcolm said, "So be it," and walked stiffly from the dining room into the dark hollow of the plaza night. Kearney laid a bill beside his plate, returned to the barroom, and sat at the rear, reviewing the scene, storing away his first impression of Charles Malcolm. For that was all he really had: a first impression. He needed time and much talk before he filled out the picture of such a man.

The barroom was quiet now. Shaffer was hanging over the beer taps, much the worse for wear, talking earnestly to Wintergreen. Kearney heard the little man pour forth his sorrows, the familiar cry of all who borrowed and suffered bad luck and found the note come due; it meant nothing until Shaffer began cursing Charles Malcolm in a thin, hopeless way. Wintergreen said, "Shush, Ed," and glanced worriedly at Kearney. "Have a beer to taper off. Tomorrow's another day."

"Don't want beer," Shaffer said stubbornly.

"Have one with me," Kearney said.

Shaffer stared blearily and Wintergreen frowned, the cautious look of the saloonkeeper mistrusting a stranger's largess. Shaffer said, "Thanks, I'll have Old Crow," and Kearney, looking directly at Wintergreen, shook his head and smiled. "I mean beer, Shaffer. A wise man tapers off." And speaking a few words, he created the first current of understanding between himself and Wintergreen, who quickly drew three glasses and set them on the damp walnut bartop.

"There," Wintergreen said. "You see, Ed, Mr. Kearney knows when to stop."

"Stop listening in, you mean," he said.

"That too," Wintergreen said evenly. "Don't pay Ed no mind."

"Bad year for sheep?" Kearney asked.

"Hell, everything happened to Ed," Wintergreen said. "Man ordinarily gets a little grief over five years. Ed got it all this season. I don't blame him for hitting the bottle."

"Note due?" Kearney asked.

"Tomorrow, at noon."

"To Malcolm?"

"Yes," Wintergreen said stiffly. "Don't get me wrong, it's all legal and above board, except——"

Kearney came up the bar and stood beside the stooped little man, smelled the thick, earthy sheep odor, and said, "Except this Malcolm won't give an extension like anybody else would?"

"No extension," Shaffer said sadly. "Got three hundred cash, owe him eight. Ain't got no chance."

"What's your setup?" Kearney asked.

"I'll talk, Ed," Wintergreen said. "It's like most of the boys here in the valley, Mr. Kearney. Ed's got his own place across the river in Tres Piedras country, north of the road and across from Cedar Springs. He leases grazing land from his neighbor——"

"Old Don Roberto," Shaffer put in. "Old——"

"Martinez," Wintergreen said quickly. "Big man out there. Ed hit a bad market last year, needed cash for his grazing lease. Malcolm's got the cash, now he'll get Ed's flock."

"And Martinez," Kearney said. "Won't he give Ed credit, help him out?"

"He would," Wintergreen said harshly, "but his wife and Malcolm—ah, but that's the forked tongue. I hate a man who gossips."

"You don't care much for this Malcolm," Kearney said.

"I run this bar," Wintergreen said flatly. "I don't express no sentiments for anybody in this country. I just sell my liquor and keep my mouth shut . . . when I'm using good sense."

He might have spent a week or more before he got

a toe in the door, and he had to use this opening. He caught Shaffer as the little man began sliding to the floor, lifted him easily, and carried him to the rawhide couch against the wall. Turning, he said, "This man's a friend of yours. You'll express that much sentiment?"

"He is," Wintergreen said. "Known him fifteen years."

"How much cash on him?"

"About three hundred," Wintergreen said. "You heard him spouting off."

"Then he'll need at least six hundred to be safe," Kearney said.

He opened his shirt pocket and counted off six one-hundred dollar bills and laid them on the bar.

"Make sure he pays off his note tomorrow, and have him sign a note to me. You keep it. No date of payment necessary, whatever interest you figure is fair, but no more than six per cent." He smiled faintly and made Wintergreen blush and look away. "That's good beer, you keep your pipes clean."

He was halfway to the lobby arch before Wintergreen found his voice: "Now wait . . . now look here, you just can't——"

"Why not?" he said.

"Well, hell! You don't know Ed, you don't even know me."

"Let's just say I know Malcolm," he said, and crossed the lobby and took the stairs into the upper hall darkness. He locked his door and stood at the window, watching the plaza below, tired now, suddenly greedy for sleep. He lowered the window halfway to the sill, undressed and eased into the sagging bed, laid out his holster and Colt on the chair, and began shifting over the lumps and arroyos until he struck a happy medium and let sleep claim his thoughts.

Malcolm strode viciously from the plaza into Pueblo Road, boots smashing through manure, over trash, the anger in his body at strange variance with his face, white and composed in the darkness. He heard the Indian whisper and he stopped, made his arms relax, let his rage die as Vigil and the big dog ranged beside him and waited silently.

"Well," Malcolm said. "What do you think of him?"

"Very wild," Vigil said. "Sharp eyes."

"And sharp tongue," Malcolm said reluctantly. "We'll go home. Come, Oso."

He led them up the rutted road to the silent house. The candles were lit in the back room, reflecting silver beams against the paintings, dropping pools of yellow light into the thick corners. Malcolm took his chair and rubbed the big dog's neck and stared at the wall. No one had spoken to him that way in many years, no one had thrust so bluntly through his defenses and turned them to water. And what did he think of John Kearney now, what did he see and how did he feel? He curled his fingers into the big dog's coarse hair and saw Kearney before his eyes.

He saw a man not much taller than himself, heavy-shouldered and flat in the belly, with the strong, slab-muscled legs of the horseman and the powerful hands that knew work and injury, yet were as supple as his own. But that was only the shell; that much all men possessed in one of the million varieties claimed by all men. For that, for the muscle and the body and the physical skills, Malcolm had the purest contempt; but not for the face and the tongue and the mind behind that face. He remembered the unkempt corn-colored hair that framed the weather-browned face, the block of jaw and firm mouth and yellowish teeth, the lumpy, once-broken nose and the crescent scar across the right cheek; and then the eyes, dark to the edge of blackness beneath the thick-boned porch of brow and forehead. The man, in his rough clothes, was deceiving. He aped a hundred others who had come and gone in Taos, cattlemen, miners, riders passing through, all a blended part of the land. But Kearney's tongue gave the lie to all that. Rough, yes, but not the same. How sharp he could only guess, but tonight was the second time in six years that any man had recognized Shakespeare and thrown it back in his teeth. And the eyes while the tongue formed words—they had bitten into Malcolm and torn his façade to shreds.

Yet all this was nothing, even the sudden shock of exposure as Kearney recited the past to him, bell, book and candle. He could remember the Nebraska couple, the daughter who came begging in the night, the con he used; but he could not remember their faces, their words, the house they lived in. He had passed briefly, made his score, and gone on; and they merged with others in a gallery of fools who vanished twenty-five years and countless miles in the past—and he wanted no more truck with their ghosts. Anyone else coming—he could handle that sort of business, but Kearney was different. Kearney had sat at the table, ready for anything, probably carrying a shoulder gun and eager to try his luck. Kearney cared nothing about the money; that was incidental. Kearney was carrying the memory of a girl he could scarcely have known, having been gone ten years, yet he had dropped whatever he did and come riding into Taos like Galahad on a white horse.

"No other way," Malcolm said. "Vigil."

"Yes, *patrón*?"

"Take care of him," Malcolm said. "Tonight is best, he will not expect trouble so soon. What room has he?"

"The big one," Vigil said. "In front."

"Rachel is working tonight," Malcolm said. "Use her if need be. But no guns."

"No, *patrón*."

"How will you do it?" Malcolm asked.

"Roof," Vigil said. "Through the window."

"Into the bed?" Malcolm said. "No, not in the dark, not through blankets."

"No," Vigil said quietly. "I'll use her, at the door. Then through the window."

"He might light the lamp," Malcolm mused.

"No matter, *patrón*."

He considered it thoughtfully, his mind mostly concerned with the girl, Rachel. She had come to his house for three months whenever Vigil brought her the command; and three months was just one week beyond his self-imposed limit for any woman in the valley. But she would listen, and obey, and tomorrow she could be sent to the ranch.

"However you wish," he said. "If you use her, she is to leave for the ranch with you as soon as you finish."

"Yes, *patrón*."

"Do it then," he said, and lowered his head and did not look up until he sat alone in the room.

Kearney heard the tapping in the far, sleep-swaddled distance; it made him burrow deeper into the blankets before he swam upward from dreamless sleep. He felt night wind cool across his face, he heard the knock and reached for the Colt.

"Yes?" he said.

"Señor, I must see you," she called softly.

"Who is it?" he asked.

"Rachel," she said. "I served you tonight, señor."

He said, "One moment," and laid the Colt on the chair. He swung from bed on the wall side and stood naked on bare feet, shivering as the night wind swept his body. He swore softly and lifted the blankets from the bed and draped them tentlike around his neck and went around the foot of the bed to the door and pulled the chair away, feeling the wind curl beneath the blanket canopy and chill his thighs. He said, "In a minute," and found the knob; and as he opened the door he heard a soft sound from the window and felt the blow against the blankets. He jerked the door open and caught her arm before she could leap away. He pulled her inside, slammed the door, and dove for the chair. He scooped up his Colt and rolled against the wall beside the window and saw the rope outlined thin in the night sky, jerking wildly as it vanished into the darkness above; and feet pattered softly on the dirt roof. Kearney said, "Don't move," and dug for his coat. He found a match and lit the lamp; in the spreading light he faced the girl who pressed against the closed door and stared at him in terror. Kearney held the Colt in one hand and swung the blankets around his body until he found the knife, buried in the loose folds, hilt deep, driven through three blankets before its force was spent.

"All right," he said. "Let's have a little talk."

"I did not know——"

"Your name?" he said.

"Rachel Perez," she said. "Señor, I must go."

Kearney tossed the knife onto the chair: a plain store butcher knife sharpened and weighted for throwing, just one of a thousand identical knives beneath the hammered lead.

"I ought to use it on you," he said quietly. "Setting me up this way. Now tell me you didn't know he was outside the window."

"Señor," she whispered. "I did not know . . . did someone throw the knife?"

"Someone didn't bring it to carve a chicken," he said. "Someone told you to knock, Rachel. Who?"

"No, señor," she said. "I did not know of this."

"It was just me, eh?" Kearney said. "You served the beans and beef, you just couldn't resist me. You had to come up and tell me how much you cared, bless your sweet loving little heart——" he crossed the room and touched her cheek with the Colt barrel. She was young and round, she had a fine smile when she used it in safer places. He hadn't noticed her during supper, but he saw her now, and the thoughts moved quickly as he judged her beauty by the standards of her people and knew she was far above the average.

"It wasn't him," Kearney said easily. "He's no monkey. So it was someone close to him. What's the Indian's name, Rachel?"

"Vigil," she said, and covered her mouth in sudden anger at her own stupidity.

"Don't feel bad," he said. "It had to be him. Rachel, you know what I can do to you? Listen closely, little one. Answer a few questions and you can go. Vigil told you to knock on my door, get me up. What were you to do next?"

"Please, señor!"

"You poor little fool," Kearney said. "Do you think I'm a damn gringo greenhorn? I live where the mother tongue is still pure, on the river in the Big Bend. I've known a hundred like you, Rachel. My friends then, my friends still. You don't lie well, Rachel. You've been going to him, no? Sure, it's in your eyes so bright you blind me. And after tonight you'd not stick around here either. He gave you orders to leave. Where . . . quick, say the words!"

"The ranch," she said. "I go to the ranch."

"Where is that?"

"Below Questa," she said. "Along the lower canyon of the Red before it enters the river."

"What name?"

"How you say it . . . John Bull."

"It would be," he laughed softly. "All right, go your way, Rachel. I'll not talk of tonight."

She stood unmoving until he opened the door and pushed her into the hall, and, closing the door, he saw her face in a spray of lamplight, frightened and wondering, filled with the first doubt. That was worth the closeness of it all: to place doubt in someone near to Malcolm. Kearney jammed the door, pushed the bed deeper into the corner, and spread out the blankets. He laid the knife beside his Colt and smoked for an hour before sleep came again, thinking almost happily of tomorrow noon when he intended to be an interested observer of the scene between Ed Shaffer and Malcolm.

# Chapter Two

TO a fiscally ruined man, his bank was the most oppressive place in the world. One might logically suppose the air of oppression was most native to a courthouse where men lost, not money or property, but freedom and life itself. Yet it seemed such losses meant less in the human scheme than signing over land and animals to satisfy past-due notes. Sheriff Montez had pondered that riddle for years, and, having been a witness to Ed Shaffer's note-signing in the spring, he entered the bank at noon with grave reluctance. How many times had Malcolm collected in six years? Montez had lost count.

"Good morning, sheriff," Kearney spoke.

Montez had approached the bank head down; now he found Kearney and Ed Shaffer flanking him with broad smiles. How could a man laugh when his flock was lost? Montez said gloomily, "With your permission?" and preceded them inside where Kearney veered to the teller window and Shaffer walked briskly toward the bullpen rail. Charles Malcolm waited behind the rail, resembling the wrath of God. Malcolm was not famous for bubbling spirits but he should be smiling upon a lugubrious Shaffer.

"Another unhappy moment," Montez said.

"Yes," Malcolm said. "Well, Shaffer?"

"Now we get to the easy, painless way of paying off my debt," Ed Shaffer laughed.

"Don't joke," Malcolm said. "Just sign these papers."

"What happens then?"

"We settled that yesterday," Malcolm said curtly. "You sign over title to your flock."

"Let's see," Shaffer said. "At your usual low rate of twenty per cent interest, that's eight hundred and eighty dollars for the six months. Here's your money, Malcolm. Mark that note paid and fork it over."

Montez saw the look of utter surprise on Malcolm's face, saw the gray eyes shift and followed their gaze to Kearney at the teller window. Montez had lived and triumphed in a town famous for swift looks; it took him no longer to tie the three together. Kearney had loaned Shaffer the money, and Malcolm was guessing the connection. That brought Jack Wintergreen into the play, for Jack and Shaffer were *amigos,* and the grapevine told of Shaffer's drinking last night in Kearney's presence. Now Malcolm was holding an empty sack. The sheriff's first impulse was to swear in six more deputies and prepare for the worst. He withdrew a respectable pace as Ed Shaffer took the note and ripped it into jagged pieces.

"I congratulate you," Malcolm said dryly. "You have hidden resources."

"No," Shaffer said. "Just good friends."

"Who trust you?"

"All the way," Shaffer grinned. "They know an honest face."

"Trust is a vice," Malcolm said. "Montez, sorry to waste your time. I knew nothing of this development."

"For nothing," Montez said. "It was no trouble."

Kearney turned from the teller window, pushed a yellow deposit slip into his shirt pocket, and crossed the room. Charles Malcolm said, "I see you intend to stay, Kearney."

"I do?" Kearney smiled.

"Opening an account," Malcolm said. "I thought you might wait until tonight to decide."

"Made up my mind last night," Kearney said. "Decided there were too many opportunities I just couldn't turn down. How are you today, Ed?"

"Just fine, John," Shaffer said happily.

"Let's eat," Kearney said. "Sheriff?"

"Another time," Montez said.

"You, Malcolm," Kearney said. "Or don't you eat out on certain days?"

"Is today a certain day?" Malcolm asked.

"Well," Kearney said. "I hear that Vigil does your cooking, and him being out of town and all . . ."

Montez tasted the currents running harsh and salty, read a variety of meaning in the idle words. He said gracefully, "Adios," and retreated to the general store porch where he saw Kearney and Shaffer enter the hotel while Malcolm walked swiftly across the plaza for home. Then Montez went to the kitchen door of the hotel and beckoned the cook.

"Is Rachel working today?"

"Quit again," the cook said grumpily. "Damn these girls. Get a dollar ahead and lay off a month." The cook gnawed his soup-stained thumb with a leer, his meaning more significant than his words.

"Thanks," Montez said.

He walked to the courthouse, closed his office door, and called Carlos Ramos from the inner room.

"Trouble," Carlos said. "You need me, Adolfo?"

"Carlos," the sheriff said, "you and I, we've been friends a long time. I overlook the little things because I understand your problems. Your pay is small, our county is unable to raise salaries, a man must do as his conscience directs. You understand?"

"Yes, Adolfo."

"Then answer me truthfully," Montez said. "Did you overhear my talk with Kearney yesterday?"

"Well," Carlos said awkwardly, "yes, I did, Adolfo."

"And you passed that news to Malcolm," Montez said. "Wait now, I am not angry. I know he pays you for those little tidbits. I don't say stop because I also know you never tell him those things which might hurt justice. Did you tell him, Carlos?"

"Adolfo, I saw no harm . . ."

"There was none," Montez said. "But from this day, Carlos, swear on the memory of your sacred mother, my sister, that you will not say one word to Malcolm before you see me first . . . do you swear it, Carlos?"

"I swear it," Carlos said. "But honest to God, Adolfo, I meant no harm."

"I know," Montez said. "Now go have a beer and let me think."

Alone, the sheriff scratched his curly hair in perplexity. He remembered Kearney's letters, one from the governor, another from the U.S. marshal, both recommending Kearney in the highest terms and asking—thus hiding the order in a velvet glove—the sheriff to co-operate in any and all ways pursuant to Kearney's business in Taos. Carlos had raced up the alley and earned another handful of dirty dollars. Then Malcolm came to the inn, spoke with Kearney, others watched and passed the word of bad blood between them; then Kearney was seen with Wintergreen and Shaffer in the barroom, and everyone knew Shaffer had lost his flock to Malcolm. Something had happened last night, Shaffer paid off today, Kearney opened an account, and Rachel Perez was missing.

"By God!" the sheriff said hopelessly. "These gringos —don't they ever do anything the simple way?"

Oso growled warning when Malcolm entered the back room. He faced the kitchen door, knowing before he entered that Oso's respected enemy was presiding over the cookstove.

"Hello, Carlitos," she called. "Come in, come in!"

She was stirring the iron pot, her flat back arched beneath her gray cotton dress, thin legs spread wide and moccasined feet planted firmly on the floor. Her long hair was a black fan across her shoulders, hiding the sharp blades and backbone ridge, her angularity an insult to all soft, round womanhood. She poured stew into bowls and turned with a smile. Her face could smile, plunge into anger, show compassion, affect pity, all in an instant; her true thoughts were hidden as deeply as his own. Sweat glistened in the pockmarks that scarred her white cheeks and cleft her chin; her eyes lay deep-socketed, sooty and shining; she looked the very image of a witch on earth. Which was not surprising, for Teresita McKinley was the most powerful *bruja* in the upper valley.

"I did not expect you back today," Malcolm said.

"Vigil is gone," Teresita said. "And who would cook your dinner?"

"I'm not hungry," he said stiffly.

"You are," she said. "Sit . . . eat . . . you are troubled."

"Nothing," Malcolm said. "A business deal gone wrong."

"The little sheepman," she said. "Shaffer?"

"Yes," he said. "Shaffer paid off."

She served the stew with a slice of bread off the hard loaf and the honeycomb for flavor. She poured coffee, took the other chair, rested her pointed chin in her hands, and regarded him solemnly. She had been traveling down the river the past week in Española, Chimayo and Velarde, she had just returned, yet she read his thoughts and seemed to know his trouble, a discomforting talent she was accomplishing far too often the past year.

"You had a successful trip?" he asked.

"Very profitable."

"And just returned," Malcolm said. "Yet you say I have trouble?"

"The news came to me, Carlitos."

"By broomstick, no doubt."

"Through the night," she said gravely.

Malcolm snorted. "My dear woman, drop the mask. It is unnecessary to carry your role beyond self-deception."

"It is no mask," she said. "You know I have the *poder*, the touch. Have I not proved it a hundred times?"

"You've got the power," Malcolm smiled, "and we've got the brains. That's why we're so good together, eh? But be practical—what's up your sleeve?"

How many times had they begun a new venture with those words? Reviewing the years, he remembered his first weeks in town, buying the old house, moving cautiously, creating the air of mystery he needed. She had come one night and brought the Indian with her. He knew her by name and reputation, had already considered the value of joining forces. She was a famous *bruja*, a witch whose feats were legend from Santa Fe to San Luis. She sold charms, she placed curses, she wielded a heavy stick over gullible people, her words to them lay just below God and exactly on par with the devil. From that first night of immediate understanding they had gone on to many profitable deals, working on the people with combined talents. Malcolm had considered himself past master of the con, but Teresita McKinley had shown him tricks not visualized in his wildest dreams. She placed a curse on someone; he chanced by later when the curse was working strongly and the victim near the breaking point; and he was the kind man who offered aid. How carefully he built the poor fools up, how he consoled them, promised to plead with the witch and make her remove the curse! For years the valley had believed them mortal enemies, the bad witch and the good Englishman. How he struggled with her in secret until she lifted a curse; and if the lucky person chose to reward him . . . who was he not to accept and split with Teresita? From the simple art of curse-placing and lifting they had progressed to land deals and animals, to acquisition of the ranch and the mine, to the money sacks growing fatter every month. And still, despite the fact she rarely bothered to visit him at night, people believed them mortal foes.

"Well," he said. "What have you, Teresita?"

"Nothing for now," she said. "Now that Shaffer has paid you."

"And nothing here."

"No?" she said. "There is a stranger in town. He threatens you. Don't lie, I know of this man from your past. I have not seen him but I will, then I can say how dangerous he is."

"What will you do to him?" Malcolm smiled. "Put the curse on his head?"

She was completely practical at times. She laughed and shook her head in vigorous denial, and the earrings jangled beneath the long black hair. "On a gringo like him? I'll waste no curses. There are better ways, no?"

"If needed," Malcolm said.

"So you admit he brings trouble?"

"He does," Malcolm said. "But there is no hurry, Teresita."

"Where is Vigil?"

"The ranch."

"But why?" she said. "He is not needed there . . . wait, I forget. It has been a long time for Rachel Perez. You tire of her. Vigil has taken her to the ranch. Is she causing trouble, shall I speak to her?"

"She's at the ranch," Malcolm said. "Causing no trouble. Let her alone."

She rose from the table and moved silently to the back door. The big dog watched her until she smiled and did something—Malcolm could never catch the movement or sound—and rumbled softly as he backed away.

"If you need me," she said, "I am at home."

"I'll let you know," Malcolm said.

"Poor man," Teresita smiled. "Lonely already. Who will warm your bed tonight? Your pimp is gone, you are alone. Shall I save you from those bad dreams?"

"Please," he said wearily. "Not that again, Teresita. It must stay as always."

"Then good day," she said, and was gone.

She had agreed in the very beginning that bed partners made bad business partners; but she knew, as any woman knew, that Malcolm would never willingly take her. So it had become a surface game, a play of expected words, while the resentment and desire grew within her. To take him was the first step in capturing his body, his mind, his very life; and he would never allow that. The time to end everything was coming; some day not far distant now.

"Well, old man," he said. "Business as usual?"

The big dog growled happily and pushed against his leg. Oso weighed a hundred and thirty pounds, stood ready to battle the world at his command. Oso trusted him, Vigil, and Teresita in varying degrees. For him it was love, for Vigil a kind of mutual animal understanding, but for Teresita it was fear of the unknown she somehow transmitted to the great dog.

"You agree?" Malcolm said. "Very well, old man. Let's concentrate on this business at hand."

Kearney walked east up Taos Canyon road after dinner, past Carson's old house now sagging into ruin, over the slight ridge and down the slope between a double line of cottonwoods that led toward the shadowed canyon mouth and the trail to Moreno Valley, Ute Park, Cimarron, and Raton. Taos Creek broke from the canyon and traced a serpentine, willow-marked course along the south side of town, to join lower down with Pueblo Creek and combine in a last furious rush to the river. Kearney spoke to an old man laboring beneath a sack of grain, tasted hay grass in the damp bottom, smoked in cottonwood shade, and followed the creek bank to the livery barn south of the plaza.

He picked a brown horse, made the hostler replace the latigo strap on the barn saddle, and rode southwest beside the creek, Talpa ridge and Ranchos to the south, Ranchitos under his feet. He circled north for a glance at the pueblo and came down toward town again on a worn path that crossed irrigation ditches and wound past low houses and between pole corrals. He stopped for a blow and his first look at Malcolm's back wall, standing the brown horse opposite a small, neat adobe house; his coming brought a woman who shaded her eyes and smiled. Her voice was soft and musical, her teeth long and white in the sad mask of face.

"Good day, mister."

"Good day, madam," Kearney replied politely.

"Miss," she corrected.

"How sad," Kearney smiled. "You are making many fine bachelors unhappy."

"At my age?" she laughed. "But you speak treasured

words to a hopeless woman. And you are strange to our town. You speak the mother tongue as I have heard it to the south."

"But poorly," Kearney said. "Cowpen style, Big Bend fashion, miss."

"Ah, you live where the river runs deep."

He nodded and nudged the horse forward, puzzled by the voice that charmed and the face that denied all beauty. "Good day," he said.

"Good day, Mr. Kearney."

"You know my name?"

"All will know your name soon," she said. "A prince comes to challenge the king who trembles on his throne."

He saw the malice in her face, the smile that curled the white, pock-marked cheeks. He said, "Your name, if I may know?"

"My poor name?" she laughed. "Teresita McKinley, a maiden of many years humbly at your service."

He tipped his hat and rode beside Malcolm's high wall to Pueblo Road, and south through town to the livery barn. He went directly to the hotel barroom and interrupted the checker game.

"Who the devil is Teresita McKinley?"

"You met her?" Wintergreen asked.

"Just now," he said. "A funny one, eh?"

"Not funny," Wintergreen said. "She takes some explaining. I guess it'll take both of us."

It took them half an hour before the woman stood three-dimensional in his mind. "So she sets them up," he said, "and Malcolm saves their souls?"

"Nobody admits it," Shaffer said, "but that's the truth. I've been across the river a long time, I know a dozen had the curse put on 'em and paid their last cent to Malcolm to get it lifted. She's a damn traitor to her own people, that's what she is."

"They've worked together since he came here?"

"From the start," Wintergreen said. "Lifting curses is just a sideline now. He's got the ranch, a mine, and nobody knows what else."

"Three of them," Kearney said softly. "Malcolm, the

33

woman, and Vigil. Thank you, boys. That's good to know."

"I never stick my long nose into private affairs," Wintergreen said. "But after what you done for Ed, and the way you're acting, it appears you might need help. We just want you to understand how we feel in that regard. All you need to say is the word."

"Don't jump, then look," Kearney said. "If I rang you into my deal, you'd have to understand the whys and wherefores. Maybe it's best if you never know."

"Can't be that bad," Wintergreen said. "I admit we ain't the best, but we know this country and we're not exactly cripples."

"That's the point," he said. "You live here, work here, got to get along. I could cut all that like a stacked deck."

"Let us be the judge," Wintergreen said.

"I've got nothing to lose," Shaffer said. "Nothing I didn't gain this noon, thanks to you."

Kearney made his decision in that moment. He could go on alone and waste days, even weeks, or he could place his trust in these men and hope for the best.

"I'll see you tonight," he said. "You can come in or stay out. All I ask is respect for my privacy."

He went outside and lingered in the shade, holding all he had learned in the cup of his mind, considering his next step. He'd talk with some people around the plaza, night would pass as all nights did, and tomorrow was the time.

Charles Malcolm followed an aimless pattern that afternoon. He came downtown at two and wandered about the plaza, drinking coffee, visiting the stores, the courthouse, the bank, loafing with the old men in the shade. All through that afternoon he caught glimpses of Kearney who, like himself, was apparently following an aimless course. Malcolm returned home to feed the dog, hoping Vigil might arrive to cook supper; but Vigil was late and the kitchen held no charms. Malcolm dressed for dinner, walked to the hotel, and surveyed the available tables. Kearney was eating alone, served tonight by a new girl. Malcolm went directly to that table and removed his hat with a certain emphasis.

"May I join you, Mr. Kearney?"

"Eating under false pretenses is bad for digestion."

"But we understand each other," Malcolm said. "I suggest a truce while we dine together in a civilized fashion."

"All right," Kearney said. "Take a chair."

"Thank you," Malcolm said. "I regret the lack of conveniences. Candlelight would ease our burden."

"The hell with candlelight," Kearney said. "That won't fill you up."

Malcolm laughed delightedly, ordered his meal, and shot his cuffs. He wore a gray coat over a fresh white shirt, and gray trousers of a fine, soft material. He sent the girl for a bottle of wine, spread his napkin, poured, and offered a toast.

"To the curious," Malcolm said. "See how they stare and opinionate. Nothing is secret in Taos. They know all, and knowing all cannot understand our situation."

"Maybe they do," Kearney said.

"No," Malcolm said firmly. "I know them as children with a child's quick judgments. A strange town, Mr. Kearney, a strange land."

"It's your home," Kearney said. "A man's chosen place ought not to be strange to him."

"Do you find that true . . . wherever you go, whoever you meet?"

"Yes," Kearney said. "I know my home and my people."

"You are a lucky man," Malcolm said. "Ah, dinner is served. My dear, will you remove your thumb from my plate?"

Eating, Kearney saw the blindness in the man across the table. Living was nothing more than making the shift from one kind of existence to another. He'd done it, others had, but it seemed that Malcolm cheated because he carried his own personal being from place to place. And that was worse in many ways than such men as Shaffer who, going broke, just picked up the scraps, moved on to another existence, broke completely with the past and made the best of the present. Malcolm's life was empty because Malcolm brought his own world into the personal existence of others and, instead of accepting and respecting their world at least on the surface, laughed at them and imposed his own while milking them dry. Malcolm was cheating the world but, ironically, he was cheating himself worst of all. He always had, always would, and one day when he was an old, old man—if he survived—he would find life so bleak and thin and lonely that his hell on earth would encircle him, make him yearn for death. And that was just when nature played her trump card on such a man, kept him dangling by one weak heartbeat, one half-ruptured vessel, one soft blood clot, until he felt transparent as glass and received less from life for all his fat years than the saddest, poorest man in the world.

"A penny for your thoughts," Malcolm said.

"Sorry." His coffee had cooled; Malcolm was leaning back with a cigar. He said, "Not keeping my end of the bargain."

"But you are," Malcolm said. "I dislike talk while eating. Over the port, yes, but we have no port so we'll make do."

"Too sweet for me anyway," Kearney said absently. "Had some once."

"Where?"

"Omaha," he said. "No, it was San Antonio. Association meeting."

"Cattlemen?"

"Yes," he said, and grinned, for Malcolm was extracting information in the smoothest possible way. "I'll save you the trouble," he said. "I've got a spread down there, I get along, it's where I want to live and die."

"Forgive me," Malcolm said. "I was not consciously prying——"

"I believe you," Kearney said. "You just can't help it, eh?"

"Something like that," Malcolm laughed softly. "Well, the meal is finished. Truce concluded?"

"Who knows?" Kearney shrugged. "The coffee's cold, you don't warm over the dreams."

"I enjoyed this meal," Malcolm said. "But I must be honest with you. You realize we will not sit again and break bread?"

"Not me," Kearney said.

"I quite agree," Malcolm said. "I don't know if you intend carrying on such foolish business, but as the boys say, I'll be doing business at the same old stand for many years to come. . . . Kearney, you are a nuisance. I would consider a settlement, something within reason, to get you out of town."

"No," he said. "No money now, Malcolm."

"You fool!" Malcolm said bitterly. "So be it!"

Kearney watched him go and murmured, "Why, he's worried!" and found that odd. He had done nothing yet to cause Malcolm real worry. But tonight, all in one capsule, was his key to Malcolm: it really wasn't what he had done so far; it was the past trooping outward from the shadows that caused Malcolm worry. And even knowing nothing, a man could use that past and twist it into a hangman's knot, given the time and the odd chance.

"More coffee, señor?"

"No more," he said. "Thanks."

He entered the barroom and played checkers with Shaffer until the last customer departed and Wintergreen locked the doors. He looked at them, the tall man with the red sour-mash nose, the stooped little man who carried the odor of his life on his skin. He wondered what the lawyers would say to his pick of men—a bartender, a busted sheepman! The lawyers would call him a fool, the detectives would argue sensibly that neither had the qualifications for this job, let alone trusting them. But his uncle, a simple man, would say, "If you trust them, what else matters?" Well, he knew their kind and he trusted them. Kearney sat with them at the back table and began talking. He plowed through it all, held nothing back, and said finally, "Now take your choice."

"He did all that?" Shaffer said. "Why, he's hurt a lot of innocent people, Jack."

"He has," Wintergreen said heavily. "I don't give a damn if he stole the U.S. mint, but what he did to your uncle's girl is enough. We sort of guessed some of this, John, the rest is just frosting on the cake. Deal us in. What can we do?"

"Start talking about Malcolm," Kearney said. "Spread the news he's wanted back East. Tell more of it to men you trust. . . . How many could we count on in the pinch?"

"I can name you twenty-five he's hurt," Wintergreen said, "and fifty more who hate the ground he walks on. I'll handle the speechifying. What else?"

"Tell me about Don Roberto Martinez," Kearney said. "He's had dealings with Malcolm, eh?"

"That takes some explaining," Wintergreen said. "Don Roberto is a big man across the river, a real old-timer, runs his place like the old days. He says jump, everybody kicks the cow over the moon. He runs sheep, he lives to himself, just like it was before the gringos took over."

"How old is he?" Kearney asked.

"Fifty-odd," Wintergreen said. "Two sons and a daughter by his first wife. He got married again three years ago. This second wife is only about thirty, just a little older than his daughter. And according to the gossip—Ed, you tell it. You know 'em all."

"Well," Shaffer said reluctantly. "There's talk that Teresita McKinley knew Maria—she's the second wife—over around Cimarron, that Teresita introduced her to Don Roberto and got him all tangled up. The two boys—Isidro and Miguel—are both at home, but they stay out of things around the house. The daughter, she hates Maria because she can see what's going on. Teresita comes visiting all the time, and Malcolm is out there a lot more than he ought to be. I don't listen much to sheep-camp talk but now I've heard you, John, I'd put nothing past Malcolm. I don't know what it is, but something is going on out there."

"Has Don Roberto got the cash?" he asked.

"Plenty," Shaffer said. "Cached away too, like they all keep it."

"I want to call on Don Roberto," Kearney said. "Ride out to your place, then go over. You can tell him I'm backing you, we want to increase your flock and we need more graze. Will that do?"

"Yes," Shaffer said. "But don't hurt his daughter. She's a fine girl, that Flavia."

"I wouldn't hurt anyone," Kearney said, "but you know how it goes. Jack, you start those rumors."

"You bet," Wintergreen said. "This way we might get him riding pretty high on the browband, eh?"

"I hope," he said. "Now I'd like to leave tonight and be back in three days. Can we do that, Ed?"

"Back in two," Shaffer said. "If you can stand my cooking that long."

"I'll try anything once," he smiled. "Jack, don't get into trouble."

"I'll be generous," Wintergreen said. "I'll save it all for you."

Teresita McKinley came to the house at midnight, slipped through the back wall gate, and tapped softly on the kitchen door. Malcolm held the big dog back when she entered, and she moved across the table behind the reading lamp, her face in shadow, her hands hidden in the heavy *rebozo*.

"I am sorry," she said, "but it was necessary to come tonight."

He had been drinking, she knew, seeing the redness in his eyes, the slack jaw line and trembling hands. He never staggered, his tongue did not thicken until the second bottle, and even deep in brandy he seemed to absorb the raw smell rather than exude it.

"Important, no doubt," Malcolm said. "Your broomstick is broken, you need a new switch?"

"I have news," she said calmly. "Concerning Kearney."

"Well, bless you," Malcolm said, and she knew he was deep into the second bottle for his iron control slipped and his tongue played a fuzzy game with his words. "Tell me secrets I don't know. What color is his underwear, does he shave with a straight razor——"

"He left tonight," she said. "With Shaffer."

"That is important news?"

"Think," she said. "Would he visit a sheepman? No, he will visit Don Roberto."

"Out of my sight for a few days," Malcolm said. "Good riddance."

"Think," she said again. "You did not tell me all you knew about this man. I lost time, I must gather my own information. I know why he has come, Carlitos. He comes to ruin you, and you call it little trouble? What happened at the hotel last night? Why is Rachel at the ranch, why is Vigil gone? You let this man walk free and you are a fool."

"That'll do," Malcolm said harshly.

"No, it will not do. Listen, this man must not become friendly with Don Roberto. I am going to Don Roberto's in the morning. If you are wise, you will follow me. And if you are sober, you will talk tonight and we will plan this business."

"What can he do?" Malcolm said. "The old man will kick him off the place."

"Hah!" she said. "He is riding with Shaffer, who knows the gossip of all Tres Piedras. Don Roberto chooses to ignore such gossip, being such a great man, such a *patrón*, such a *rico* of the first generation. We have spent three years fattening our Don Roberto for the right moment—and this man can smash it all in a day! Who cares if Don Roberto might at last feel his horns? That is nothing, Carlitos. The Martinez ranch and the mine are *everything*. Now will you talk?"

Malcolm shivered beneath his rough brown robe and pressed both hands against his cheeks. She stood implacable until he rose and walked uncertainly toward the small inner room that served as bath. He said thickly, "Give me ten minutes," and plunged through the narrow door. She heard the water splashing and turned to the stove. Making coffee, warming stew, she smiled and hummed a tune beneath her breath. She could count this as a momentous night, for at last she had imposed her will, she had shaken him. She must thank John Kearney, in some way, for doing what she had never before accomplished.

They rode northwest from Taos across the loma and swung beside the invisible gash of Arroyo Hondo and followed its deepening canyon to the bottom of the river gorge where light came only at the moon's pale zenith. The gorge was deep, a thousand feet of receding walls, of old magma hardened and erupted through all of time, thrown upward into the strata of varicolored rock, then cut and worn by the river, by the rain and the wind and time. Kearney was at home beside that river in the night; a thousand miles downstream he knew the same river as it passed the great canyons—Santa Helena, Mariscal, Boquillas—and fought its way to the gulf.

"Low," Ed Shaffer said. "We need rain."

"We always need rain," he said. "Is that the bridge?"

"Yes."

The bridgeman was asleep and missed his toll. They crossed on the loose timbers that boomed hollow under the hoofs, and climbed the switchback trail to the Tres Piedras plateau and turned north along the river, riding rough uneven country sprinkled with juniper and piñon. Shaffer led him into a clearing at first dawn when sheds and cabin lay milky gray against the earth. They had come fifteen miles to the river, and twelve miles north, and the horses grunted deep when they uncinched.

"Excuse the house," Shaffer said. "It looks like a wild sow's nest before pigging time, but a man gets careless by himself."

They turned the horses into the corral and went to the cabin, built snug against a rock outcropping. Shaffer lit the lamp and wasted no steps beginning breakfast, blowing up a fire in the cookstove, putting on cold beans, bacon, eggs, biscuits, and molasses. The cabin was untidy but the smell was clean and the dirt floor had been swept before the self-styled dirty little man rode for town. As they ate, they stretched their legs under the table, and Shaffer said,

"Martinez's is ten miles west."

"And Malcolm's?" Kearney asked.

"Across the river where the Red comes in, up the Red

in Questa valley below the town. His land lays between the Red and the Rio."

"And his mine?"

"Up Red River Canyon in the Cristos," Shaffer said. "Far up, about twenty miles from Questa."

"Let's call on Don Roberto," Kearney said. "Then I'd like a quick look at his ranch."

"All right," Shaffer said, "but I'm still worried. I don't give a damn much about him or the rest of his tribe, but Flavia is a good girl. I'd hate to see her get hurt."

"Nothing's happened yet. I'll just palaver. That can't hurt her."

"Maybe not," Shaffer said, "but I get a funny feeling just watching you. You've guessed that Maria is playing fast and loose with Malcolm, and Teresita and Malcolm have got the old man all but charmed like a snake on a bird."

"Then stay here," he said. "I'll go over."

"No," Shaffer said. "I bought in, I stay in. Let's wash up and ride."

Kearney carried water from the spring, helped wash the dishes, and rode with Shaffer to the west, on gradually rising country through thickening stands of pine. They were in sheep country where the grass came torturously from the rocky earth, sheep and horse country from the beginning of time as the Rio Arriba country measured time: from the day of the Spaniard to the present—October, 1912. They mounted a long slope and, from the ridgetop in a pool of chilled shade cast by the old bull pines, Kearney looked down on the valley where grass was greener and water flowed white from a spring in the great upthrust rocks that named the country and formed a windbreak for the big house built in its square around the inner patio.

"Hold up a spell," he said.

He dismounted and squatted beneath a pine and smoked, studying the scene below. Shaffer stood, bearded and grubby, yawning now, squinting against the cloudless blue sky. A whole small world was below them, the big house built of rock and adobe and timbers cut from these pines; the smaller houses stringing out along the spring creek, the outbuildings and sheds and corrals, the trails fanning out from the hard-packed yard to all the compass points. Here was the center of one man's self-made world, for Don Roberto was no inheritor of family name and fortune and endless lands. He had begun in a sheep camp and built his world with his hands and his mind in less than a lifetime, and no man of his race was prouder than the man who lifted himself to that station in this country. His was no generationed hacienda but he had built it to house a dozen generations to come, low and thick and strong, the rooms all facing inward on the patio, the chapel in one corner, the roofed porches supported by the wooden pillars and the scrolled corbels. He would have a big room, a *sala,* and his storerooms would be crammed with food, the meat and game, the dried fruit and grain, the few provisions he bought in town now that all the land was slowly changing. The walls would be painted with gypsum with dadoes in some bright color, and while he would not possess the old furniture and the fine materials handed down from other days, he would have each room furnished richly and heavily, heavy wood and heavy materials, for his luxuries, like his life, had a heavy weight that would touch his shoulder through all the days he lived. He would have it all in his own way, some of the old and a good deal of the new, the chests and drapes and beds, the copper bowls and pottery, the glassware, perhaps the silver. And his wife would wear fine clothes and own a few jewels, upholding her part of that inward living world. He would never be *gente de razón,* not Don Roberto, but he would be giving it the best try he knew how. Watch the sheep, raise the goats, the horses, the few cattle, eat well and work hard and sleep deep, celebrate the feast days and the marriages, baptize the babies, live as long as God allowed, and then build the coffin from the fresh pine wood.

"Clean place," Kearney said.

"He won't allow dirt," Shaffer said. "He don't use a whip or his fists. He's a good man, and he's got just two faults."

"I know," Kearney said.

And he did know, looking down on the house, for these people were no different from those along the lower river. They brought the old traditions intact through the centuries, the traditions of honesty and faith and kindness, of friendship and courage and fear of God; and with the good was the bad, inseparable forever in their blood. A man must have women, and a man who amassed wealth reached out for more wealth, not so much in greed as in a way of life he could not change. Don Roberto Martinez would be a rough man, lacking the fine manners of the true *gente,* hot-blooded and acquisitive, a man who took what he saw with honest force and expected all others to be his own kind. A man who had three children and wanted more, and took another wife because he was still young. A man who could not visualize casual adultery in his own house, yet living as he did in such a way of life where, all around him, that way of life went on.

"Yes," Kearney said softly. "I know. Let's go down."

# Chapter Three

THE big house woke early those bright fall mornings. Don Roberto came to breakfast, then Isidro and his family, but they were not the earliest risers. Flavia had already taken her ride, her look at morning sky, before she joined them. Only the señora was absent, having chocolate in bed before she dressed and ate alone; but she was only a minor irritant in the smooth-running household, a passing cloud in the lives of all. One fine day she'd be gone, and the next day forgotten. In the meanwhile—here was Don Roberto, stomping and acting fierce, here was sober Isidro and his family, and here was Flavia who loved them all and held their returned love gently as a lamb. Now everybody was eating, the sun was up, the day had begun.

"Eat more, Flavia," Don Roberto growled. "You're too skinny."

"Eat less, Father," Flavia said gently, "you are too fat."

"Bah!"

He always spoke those words to Flavia. He growled at

everyone to hide his kindness. He was a stocky man with heavy legs and short arms, his shaggy buffalo head close on his thick shoulders. He tried to hide a peso-sized bald spot atop his curly black head; his eyes peered from craggy brows and fat cheek pouches of wrinkled, leathery skin. He walked with dignified, bandy-rooster steps and looked far more imposing on a horse. He was born to a horse and spent most of his waking hours astride his fine mares; and the mares betrayed his almost foolish tenderness and regard for woman, although with that half-blind veneration he was a strong man in his bed. That was his right, but also his weakness. His other weakness was an inseparable part of his life: he had worked for all he owned, he could not get enough money to repay him for those lean, terrible years, he would never blot out the agony of early poverty. He mistrusted banks, even aware of the change in the country during his fifty-five years. He kept accounts in Taos and Santa Fe but those were tokens, lip service to the changing times. The bulk of his fortune was stored in the big house, in a place known only to him. He seldom bothered to count his money; it was simply that the weight was an assurance of his worth.

He was a product of his people and his times, but then again, he was a stubborn individualist. He attended church as a duty, he was not overly superstitious, but he understood why Teresita McKinley was a necessary evil in the land. Deep in him, clinging like musk from his youth, was fear of the *bruja's* power, respect for her advice. She had introduced him to Maria—not personally but through friends in Cimarron—at exactly the proper time of his widower's existence. She had touted Maria as a fine woman, a mother of sons, a worthy mistress of his house; but he was not fooled by Teresita or Maria. She wished him to believe she came from fine people and he allowed her that harmless masquerade, for all he needed was her body. He had fifteen years or so to beget more children, and Maria was a good, strong, receptacle for the job. But with this rough, practical attitude, he was too trusting and tender. Malcolm was a welcome guest and the thought never crossed his mind that Malcolm came for any other reason. Don Roberto was vaguely unhappy these days. Three years had blessed him with no sons, and it was not his fault. Malcolm and Teresita were pressing him steadily toward the biggest transaction of his life—a trade of his river land for a half interest in Malcolm's mine—and while he sensed a huge profit he still hung back. Maria urged him to make the trade; then they could move to town, build a great house, and lord it over everyone. Flavia was his pride, his greatest joy, but Flavia ignored her stepmother and would never move to town. And when would she marry? Don Roberto sat at the head of his table, frowned lovingly on his family, and ate with hearty appetite. Thank God, he had two strong sons.

Isidro was the oldest, thirty this fall, living evidence that he bred strong and true. Isidro was short and powerfully built, somewhat placid and not a little stupid, but a man who loved the ranch and did his work well. Isidro had married six years ago and already fathered five children. The most he could say for Isidro was, his son worked and begat and slept, and would continue so until the day his joints stiffened. But Miguel— there was a different rooster.

Miguel was twenty-eight, thinner and an inch taller than Isidro, quick where Isidro was slow, suspicious where Isidro was trusting. Miguel was absent today, as he was six days of seven each week. Miguel spent his life in the far-flung sheep camps, in the woods, on the high trails. Miguel was unmarried and seemingly cared nothing for wife and children. But Miguel was no less valuable than Isidro; together they ran the ranch like a smooth-oiled machine. And finally, there was Flavia.

Flavia Martinez lived in two worlds: her own private world, and that of the ranch around her. She gave herself unstintingly to the work that was rightfully her stepmother's, but of her private world she exposed nothing and opened no doors. Very small, very quiet, she was like a young girl, a boy in slenderness and wiry strength and eagerness to suck each day dry. Thin face, huge eyes, dark hair, nimble hands and feet; and the aliveness in her face that caught and held anyone keen enough to look beyond her meek exterior. Don Roberto laughingly called her "grandmother" for her way of handling the house, her dignity of shyness, her gentle weight upon their days. She was his pride, and his heaviest cross.

"Ah," he thought. "That Flavia!"

She had visited her aunt in Santa Fe for two months after he brought Maria home. Never in word or act did she express her feeling, but she detested her stepmother, not the woman but all the woman represented: the stealth, the ignorance, the wasted beauty, the mind that lay feeble behind the beautiful face, the casual lust and the inability to recognize love in all its wonderful lasting forms. Flavia was twenty-four, ancient for a single girl, but she bestowed only passing interest on the young men who called and went away. The young men, cruel tongues said, who were drawn by Don Roberto's wealth and not her, the little mouse. And the sad part of that was, some of the young men were worthy, some touched her aliveness and responded in kind, and she recognized a lack within herself and felt quite bad for weeks after such a young man departed. But she went about her daily life, wearing her severely plain clothing, supervising the house, the cooking, the sewing and knitting and looming. She waited for something, knowing only that she would know it when it came; and she watched over her father with all her tender, concealed strength. She smiled vaguely when he chided her appetite, ate her meal, and left the table as he spoke his usual morning words to Isidro.

"Where today?"

"North," Isidro said. "And we must go to town Saturday."

"What for?"

"Supplies," Isidro said. "Flour and——"

Flavia passed from hearing into the *sala*, sharp-eyed for dust and disturbance, quick to notice if some beloved object was out of place. She took the hallway past her stepmother's room, smelled the rich odor of chocolate, heard the woman stir lazily in bed. Maria was that rare type sprung from their people, the overripe beauty with too much of all the parts of beauty, so that the whole was very nearly overpowering. Too much body, too much face, hair so fine and silky black it seemed false. Too much of everything but brain. Maria thought with her senses, never her mind, and her senses were unhampered by trust and decency. Flavia murmured, "God forgive you, stepmother," and frowned as she stepped into the front yard facing the eastern ridge and saw the riders coming down.

"José," she said, "tell Don Roberto we have company."

"Company?" the yardman said, shading his eyes. "That's just *Cargador* Shaffer."

"And the other man?"

"Ho, wait a minute . . . that's the one I heard about in town, the one Señor Malcolm hates."

"I see," she said. "Please tell my father."

"That's the girl," Ed Shaffer said. "Ho, Flavia . . . how are you?"

"Very well, Señor Shaffer," Flavia Martinez said. "And you?"

"Fit as a fiddle."

Kearney dismounted and stood, hat in hand, while Shaffer introduced him. He extended his hand and she accepted it timidly, unused to that greeting style in her woman's world, but her fingers were strong and missed very little in her study of him from hair to dusty boots. She was a quiet one, he thought, a regular little mouse in her spotless dress and soft leather slippers, her hair brushed back simply and tied in a knot, her hands reddened from housework, a strange thing to see in women of her class.

"You ride early," she said politely.

"Last night," Kearney said, "and this morning. It's best then."

Her head lifted. "You like it at night?"

"Being alone," Kearney said, "is a blessing at times."

"Yes," she said. "A great blessing, Señor Kearney."

He felt something in her reach and touch him timidly, probe at him with hope, almost with desperation, and then Don Roberto Martinez erupted from the house, embraced Shaffer, shook Kearney's hand vigorously, and welcomed them in a deep-growling voice that led on into the office just off the front hall; and, oddly, the girl followed and stood silently behind her father's chair beside the massive carved table. Kearney sat with his dusty boots soiling a silky white kidskin rug, and Don Roberto's were scuffing up another rug dyed brilliant blue. The saint-maker had passed and left his ascetic mark, a fine *bulto* of Saint Michael in a wall niche, built like a doll in the rough, primitive fashion, all sharp angles and agonized features and stark, stiff posture.

"You like him?" Don Roberto asked.

"Oh, Saint Michael?" Kearney smiled, looking once more at the *bulto,* Michael with his sword and his scales of justice. "I know him well, Don Roberto."

"In your country?"

"The Big Bend," he said. "The lower river."

"Cattle country," Don Roberto snorted. "Well, why do you honor me today, Eduardo?"

"Business," Shaffer said. "John's one of these foolish *primos* who can't wait to spend his money . . ."

Then Shaffer was leaning forward, using his hands, explaining that Kearney was interested in going into sheep with him, leasing more graze, and naturally they were interested in knowing if Don Roberto would lease them more land along the river.

"How much land?"

"All we can get," Kearney said.

"Along the river," Don Roberto said. "North from your place, Eudardo?"

"Right," Shaffer said. "That way we can use my place as headquarters and fan out."

"And the sheep?"

"Bring them in," Shaffer said. "Or buy from you, if you can spare any."

Kearney saw the girl's fingers touch her father's shoulder, saw him pause, glance upward only with his eyes, and nod. He gave her permission to speak in a man's world, and that was very strange; but then Kearney remembered Wintergreen telling that her mother had died and she was the woman of this house until the second wife came. So there was more to her, then, than the little mouse.

"Señor," she said shyly, "there is a matter of price. Would it be paid in cash or note?"

"Cash," he said. "I don't do business on time, señorita. I always pay my way."

"And you are certain it is sheep?" she asked softly. "Not cattle?"

"I have cattle," Kearney said, "where the country is made for cattle. This country is for sheep. I would sign an agreement to that effect." He paused, running his hat brim through his fingers, studying her face, then taking his first plunge. "I've heard in Taos that some people are thinking of cattle out here."

"Who?" Don Roberto asked sharply. "And where, may I ask, when I and my friends own all the land."

"Man named Malcolm," Kearney said. "I talked to him the other night."

"Malcolm?" Don Roberto said blankly. "He spoke of cattle over here?"

"Yes," Kearney said. "Offered to throw in with me."

"Let me think this over," Don Roberto said. "I will let you know—this is what?"

"Wednesday," Shaffer said.

"We come to town Saturday," Don Roberto said. "I will see you then."

"My thanks for considering our offer," Kearney said. "With your permission I'll look at your fine place and then we'll go."

"This poor place?" Don Roberto laughed. "You waste time, but it is yours. Have you eaten?"

"Yes," he said. "And we must return to town."

He rose to shake hands, bent his head to the girl, and led Shaffer into the yard. They spent half an hour touring the sheds and corrals, and led their horses up the slope to the spring above the house. Sitting a minute, he saw the woman in the patio below, a beautiful woman staring innocently at the small fountain but fully aware of his presence.

"The wife?" he asked.

"That's her," Shaffer said. "Ain't she a pippin?"

"At a distance," he said. "We'll keep her that way."

"Look," Shaffer said. "On the trail."

Kearney saw the riders to the south on the main river road, a man and woman, coming briskly down the long valley slope. They mounted and rode north into the timber, and Shaffer said, "Malcolm and Teresita coming in."

"Good," he said. "Let's swing by his place."

Teresita McKinley saw them enter the timber as she followed Malcolm into the yard. She handed her mule to José and went straight through the house to the inner patio; behind her Don Roberto was welcoming Malcolm with unexpected coolness. That was understandable, with Kearney just departing. Then she was sitting with Maria, speaking all the silly words Maria loved, how beautiful, how fresh, how Maria was younger by the day. "And so," Teresita said. "Is all well?"

Maria nodded complacently and used the silver-backed brush on her hair. She had delayed breakfast to sit in the patio, hoping for a glimpse of the stranger. Was he young and strong, was he handsome? She saw him at the spring, watched him mount and ride away, and knew he had seen her. Only a tiny exchange but enough if he chose to call again.

"And the girl?"

"The same. I can handle her."

"Stay away from her," Teresita said. "You cannot handle her."

"I can. The ugly little fool!"

"Stay away," Teresita said softly. "You hear?"

"Oh, very well," Maria said petulantly, "but why all this fuss over the kid. She's no danger, Teresita."

"She can be," Teresita said. "Now I must join Carlitos and your husband . . . and how is he?"

"What do you mean?"

"I mean what you think of only and forever," Teresita said bitingly. "Does he visit you as always?"

"More or less."

"Which?" Teresita snapped.

"Well . . . less."

"So the bull ages," Teresita laughed. "And you grow impatient."

"Do you blame me? You told me——"

"Hush," Teresita said. "I am going now. I expect to find you later as a proper mistress of this house, properly dressed, receiving in your *sala*. Oh yes, you can visit the spring tonight. I'll see to it."

She walked swiftly to the office, where Don Roberto greeted her and swung back to Charles Malcolm. "Now again," he said. "Tell me it's all lies."

"I've told you," Malcolm said. "I have no intention of bringing cattle west of the river. Kearney is a troublemaker, a Texan, and you know *Tejanos*."

"I know them," Don Roberto said darkly, "but this one looked me in the eye."

"Do I meet your gaze?" Malcolm asked.

"Yes, man."

"Then who will you believe," Malcolm said, "a stranger reaching into your pocket, or your friend of many years?"

In the past Don Roberto would swear eternal allegiance after such words; now he studied Malcolm questioningly for the first time, a serious, calculating gaze. The scales were tipping from blind trust to puzzled doubt. Next came distrust, and that meant total failure—Malcolm would not have that.

"So Kearney agreed to signing a statement," he said, "that he'd bring no cattle across the river?"

"He did."

"I'll sign a statement," Malcolm said. "Old friend, I'll post a cash bond with you, forfeit the day you find a single cow of mine west of the river."

"Oh, enough of this," Don Roberto said. "It is good to see you—and you, Teresita. Will you stay tonight?"

"With your permission," Malcolm said. "Later we will talk of the mine." Then, carelessly, he brought the leather pouch from his coat pocket and tossed it on the table. "Last week's," he said. "All we had time for. If you are selling a few sheep we can make the usual deal." He watched the stubby fingers encircle the pouch, squeeze the gold, heft it, consider the sale of extra sheep for the raw gold that bulked so comfortably in the iron box beneath the floor. Then the fingers withdrew and made a fist.

"Wait for Isidro tonight," Don Roberto said. "We may have a few for sale."

"At your leisure," Malcolm said cheerfully. "Now, you gave me no time to inquire of your family. How is your mistress?"

"Very well."

"And your sons?"

"As usual."

"And your charming daughter?"

"Monkish as ever," Don Roberto laughed. "Come, man. Let's have a little drink to start the day."

Malcolm rose and walked easily into the day of Don Roberto. He drank, ate, talked, passed the long afternoon, took a late siesta, bathed and shaved, and advanced on the supper that forever astounded him. Roast chicken, hams, chili, peppers, piñons and raisins, blue meal tortillas, cookies, chocolate—a groaning board that defied consumption, yet nearly vanished before they pushed away and reached for the brandy. And later, alone with Don Roberto and Isidro, he heard Isidro say there were no sheep for immediate sale. Isidro retired and Malcolm again spoke of the mine and the mutual benefits of the prospective trade—one half his share in the mine for Don Roberto's river land stretching five miles west from the Rio, ten miles north and south. Don Roberto had no real need for that piece, he leased parts of it to such worthless *pelados* as Ed Shaffer for practically nothing. Why not receive a steady income from a proven mine, be assured of a good neighbor, a friend who wished to raise sheep in the old tradition? "And so," Malcolm smiled, "have you come nearer a decision?"

No, Don Roberto had given it little thought the past month. But he would seriously consider it, have a family meeting with his sons and daughter——

"And your mistress," Malcolm said gently. "You must consider her."

"Oh sure," Don Roberto said. "Well, I promise you something soon, Carlitos."

"You will never regret it," Malcolm said. "Now you are tired and it is late."

He took the hallway to the guest rooms on the far north side of the big house. That wing was dark and silent when he reached his room, but the adjacent door swung open and she spoke softly.

"Any luck?"

"I had him," Malcolm said bitterly. "I had him—and Kearney queered it for another week or two. But he comes to town Saturday. I'll close it then. Can you help it along?"

"Wait until Saturday," Teresita said. "See how it goes. If you have more trouble, then it is time to stop being polite. . . . You wish to leave early in the morning?"

"Yes, for the ranch."

"You will miss sleep?"

"Eh?" he said.

"She is waiting," Teresita said. "Good night, Carlitos. Don't disappoint her."

He entered the room, closed the heavy door, and dropped the bar in place. He sat on the deep window ledge and smoked until the house was silent, deep and black in sleep. Then he slipped through the window, made his way up the slope to the spring, and walked into her arms on the far side in the trees.

They lay on the ridge above the ranch yard through the lazy afternoon. Questa was a mile north on the bench above the river bottom; the river came from the great canyon on the northeast and wound across the valley and plunged white-purling into the lower canyon on its final run to the Rio. Rachel Perez was in and out of the house all afternoon, but the Indian did not appear until dusk when he saddled a horse and rode toward the faint yellow lights of Questa.

"Anybody else on the place?" Kearney asked.

"Just him."

"We'll go down," he said.

"Social call?"

"Not exactly," he said. "I hope we don't scare her half to death."

They waited until full dark before descending the slope. They crossed the shallow river, dismounted at the barn corner, and saw the girl's dark shadow cross the window. Kearney whispered, "You sing out," and led the way to the door.

"Hey there," Shaffer called. "Rachel?"

"¿Quién es?"

"Me," Shaffer said. "You know Ed Shaffer."

"Oh, sí," Rachel Perez called. "You are out late tonight, Señor Shaffer."

Kearney caught her arm when she opened the door. "Easy now," he said, and pushed her gently across the room to the table. She twisted and tried to run, her face wild with fear.

"What's the matter?" Shaffer said. "John won't bite you."

"Señor . . ." she said thinly.

"You are living here?" Kearney asked.

"Yes, señor."

"For how long?"

And then he understood, for her hands pressed against her dress in an unmistakable way, the hands of a woman feeling growth within her. Only a moment, then she spoke sullenly.

"Who knows . . . so long as I wish."

"No," he said. "Only until you have the baby——"

"You lie!"

"Hell," he said. "You gave it away, Rachel. So he brought you out here for two reasons, and one is having the baby, and after that? Nothing . . . out you go! But you won't be lonesome. I hear you've got plenty of company around the valley."

"A lie!"

"You want a home for the baby?" he asked. "A name? You want to carry a bastard to the fount? Stay here and you will, but I'll help you if you'll help me."

"But how, señor?"

"Can you write?" he asked.

"Yes," she said proudly. "I can sign my name."

"Then I will write," he said, "and you will sign, and Señor Shaffer will witness."

"Sign what?"

"Of that night," he said. "Your part, what Vigil attempted. Then I will see that you and your baby are cared for."

"No," she said. "He would——"

"He'll do nothing," Kearney said. "Now we will write."

He sat at the table and pulled the folded paper and pencil from his inside pocket. Shaffer said, "I'll look at the horses," and slipped outside. Kearney wrote the events of that first night exactly as they occurred, blew on the paper from force of habit, and smiled at her.

"Sign here," he said. "Your full name."

"You do not lie to me . . . you won't leave me?"

"No," he said quietly. "You have my word."

She took the pencil and bent beside him, biting her lower lip, writing her name laboriously in a childish scrawl. She had a sharp, sweet smell and her hair obstructed his vision until she straightened suddenly and whispered, "Vigil!"

The Indian stood in the doorway, Winchester centered on Kearney's chest, face impassive in the lamplight. Vigil dipped the muzzle toward the paper. "Rachel, bring it."

"Stand fast," Kearney said. "Good evening, Vigil."

"Not for you."

"But I stopped to pay my respects," Kearney said. "This is nothing—I'll be going now."

"Leave it," Vigil said. "Rachel, step away!"

Kearney rose from the chair, keeping both hands in full view above his belt. He raised his voice, "This will be a bad one, Vigil," and saw Ed Shaffer clear the threshold and smash his Colt barrel behind Vigil's ear. The Winchester clattered on the chair as Vigil dropped without sound, a crumpled heap of greasy wool and worn leather on the dirt floor. Rachel Perez screamed, and continued screaming until Kearney slapped her twice and pushed her down on the window bench. He unloaded the Winchester while Shaffer searched Vigil and tossed the knife away.

"He ain't so smart," Shaffer laughed. "He never saw me."

"For which I thank you," Kearney said. "Throw some water in his face. . . . Rachel, pack up!"

He folded the paper and tucked it safely into his coat, and dropped on one knee while Shaffer tipped the water bucket. Vigil grunted and opened his eyes, his body lax, unable to respond to nerve command.

"You know me?" Kearney asked.

"Yes."

"What do you think comes now?"

Vigil spoke in his own tongue, guttural and defiant words. Kearney pushed his left hand against Vigil's jaw and touched his Colt muzzle lightly on the flattened nose.

"No," he said. "Save the death song. We'll call it quits for now."

"Fool," Vigil said thickly. "Next time I don't miss."

"You're the fool," Kearney said. "Stay with him and you'll lose everything. Get out while there's time."

He took the girl's arm and led her outside and watched Vigil through the doorway until Shaffer saddled a horse and led all three from the corral. Then Kearney threw the Winchester far behind the cabin, boosted Rachel Perez into her saddle, and led the quick run across the river and up the slope toward the Taos road.

"Rachel, you know the sheriff?"

"Yes, señor."

"You trust him?"

"Oh, yes."

"Good," he said. "I will have him care for you."

"In jail, señor!"

"No," he laughed. "In a good house, a safe one."

Ed Shaffer laughed softly. "Montez'll have a conniption fit."

"Why?"

"The way we're spreading trouble," Shaffer said. "Taking in boarders. You'll have him wondering just what kind of bravado you are."

"A wild one," he said. "Me?"

"Yes, you," Shaffer said. "I'm wondering now myself."

Following the departure of their guests next morning, Flavia Martinez went directly to her father's office. She could not breathe freely until those two were gone, and this morning she was deeply worried.

"You spoke to Isidro?" she said.

"A little."

"But you did not call me?"

"It was nothing, child."

"Nothing?" she said, gently insistent. "Señor Malcolm is pressing you for a decision. What did you tell him?"

"Nothing," Don Roberto said. "I'll give him my answer Saturday in town."

He waited to be left alone but, as always, his daughter only folded her slender hands and gazed at him all too steadily. His conscience, he liked to call that look, meek as milk but stronger than steel, and it never failed to worry him. "Well?" he said kindly. "You're worried about something?"

"Señor Kearney," she said. "What do you think of him?"

"How can I think?" Don Roberto said. "I scarcely know the man."

"But he spoke honestly to you, Father."

"Can I read his mind?"

"But he made you think," she said. "Father, I have heard talk about Señor Kearney and Señor Malcolm. Please don't deny it—I know you talked with José. Father, I do not approve of Señor Malcolm's deal."

"Your brother does."

"One brother," she said. "You must hear Miguel too."

"He will approve," Don Roberto said. "Your mother does——"

"My mother is dead," she said firmly.

"Your *mother* does," Don Roberto said loudly. "Listen, I forced Carlitos to sweeten the pot. He will sign an agreement, post a cash forfeit bond. What more do you want?"

"Father, I do not know, but it is not right."

"In God's name," Don Roberto shouted, "why not? We don't need the river land. We never needed it."

"It was your first land," she said softly.

"Bah! I have better now."

"You do not need the gold," she said. "You never needed gold."

"Hah," Don Roberto snorted. "What has this Kearney done to you? Do you see him as knight in armor? Child, you are a very wise woman in many ways. I treasure your advice, you know that. Don't I let you listen and talk when my friends wouldn't let your left ear press a knothole? But you are no judge of men. He's just another one of those loud-talking *Tejanos*, all wind and no bottom."

"I think he is none of those," she said.

"Then what is he?"

She looked beyond her father, through the tiny window at one segment of blue sky. "I do not know, but he is not like others. Yes, Father . . . what is he?"

Vigil squatted against the wall and took Malcolm's wrath, listened to the icy voice rip him up one side and down the other. Vigil simply closed his ears, let his thoughts roam happier times, while his body stood empty and unresponsive in the present. He remembered childhood games and his mind mustered the forgotten scenes in the same manner he might speak of them in the short, jerky speech of his race where one word replaced the white man's ten. He remembered the stick game, roll the hoop, shinny with buckskin balls and hooked sticks, fishing in the creek and the river and high in Blue Lake. And school, sixteen wasted months in 1897 and 1898 before he returned to the games, the hunting, and the serious business of becoming a man: to planting with ox teams, feeding them cornstalks, to cutting wheat in the fall, first hiring Spanish people with goats to eat the grass, then water that place, circle the goats to tramp the ground solid, make a fence, put the wheat there, walk horses in a circle to separate straw from grain, then wait for wind to blow the straw away. Growing older in a changing world, wanting to live as his father before him, but caught by the gringo idea of school and commissioners, of doing things the gringo way. Having one religion from the past, and another superimposed by the Spaniards and refined by the gringos, until a man had so many gods he could not choose the strongest. Rebelling against the new, returning to the old, living apart in the high peaks, hunting and fishing and making friends with such people as Teresita McKinley, with the outcasts who could not believe in anything and thus went faithless. Passed over when his time came to serve on the council because he was judged too bronco, too wild. And he could speak and write three languages. And now, for six years, he had known a kind of contentment working for Malcolm, finding a release for his angers and his energies. He could not escape now, having tasted power, nor did he care to leave this man. He could only obey commands and realized he was changing until he was no longer Indian, Spaniard, or gringo—what was he? He did not know. All he knew was this life, to sit deaf until the cold words passed. For Malcolm spoke himself dry in a few minutes and became himself, and now it happened again.

"Well," Malcolm said. "It's done and over. We will go to town."

"Yes, *patrón*," Vigil said calmly.

"We will leave now," Malcolm said. "You follow in two hours."

"Yes, *patrón*."

Malcolm walked to his horse, glanced at Teresita as she mounted her yellow mule, and shook his head in wonder.

"Kearney?" he said softly. "What manner of man is this?"

What manner of man? A man whose life, in every way, was alien to Charles Malcolm. A man of thirty-four who would never forget childhood's lessons so that, searching back, he continually found kernels of value applicable to the present, long after the father was dead and the boy become a man. Malcolm would have been surprised to know that Kearney's father was a devout man who believed in the Bible in a peculiar, individual way, but found his devoutness mostly in a lifelong faith in his own personal honesty. He instilled those habits in his son, and the boy who began with something solid usually went on living and growing solidly. Not necessarily in approved ways—but always honest with himself. Kearney heard the Bible read at night by that stern father, yet was never ordered to take the Good Book as life's only guide, but rather as a help when written words somehow helped to solve a problem, fill a need. He went to school when weather and work permitted, he read every book in District 46, and when he left school forever upon graduation from the eighth grade he continued to read wherever he was. Malcolm would not understand the boy who matured quickly and covered a wide range of country before he was twenty-one: Wyoming, the Dakotas, but always home to Nebraska until, at twenty-four, alone, he began moving south, always south, and came at last to the Big Bend; and there, fifteen hundred miles from all the strings and habits of his youth, where he might be expected to fail utterly, go sour, or turn bad, he put down roots and found his home. Malcolm would never understand a man who chose the river itself, just above Boquillas Canyon on Screwbean Creek, in a country so wild and tough and dry that, as the story went, many a man carried his wife's shoes on his saddle to keep her at home. Kearney chose a land that gave no quarter in weather, time, or simple existence; and he prospered because he understood his surroundings and accepted them.

He started small, he built slowly, he learned another language and came to know its speakers as men, as friends, not as aliens, and he stayed alive in a land of sudden death, of robbery and treachery and cheap life —and all that was easy for no man, it was easier to slip into different ways. But he kept his own solid, lasting values, and that was hardest of all. He lived alone with his men and their women. He visited town once a year and made the most of it—a glorious drunk, a woman, talk with other men—and came home unchanged.

He saw so much of violence that he hated all killers, yet he became so proficient with rifle and Colt, so able on a trail, so sure in his grasp of country and his judgment of other men, that his Association literally pushed him into the dangerous inspection work every other year for periods of several months. And he paid the price for helping his fellow members. His reputation had grown through the years until he rode watching his backtrail, and could not forget the list of men on both sides of the river who, for one reason or another, wanted him dead. He lived through so much in those short years he would have been forgiven if he turned hard and calloused. But he escaped that callosity and kept his sense of humor—a saving grace for any man— and remained curious in all things and continued to read his tobacco coupon books, talk and live as all decent men. At times, deep in work, he was almost a stranger to himself. He wasted no sympathy on his body in those times; it was there to be used. He hoped, some day, for a home and children, but he refused the second-best. He went on alone, unhurried, certain the time would come. Malcolm would never understand how a man, ten years gone from Nebraska and the uncle scarcely remembered, could answer the uncle's plea for help. Malcolm would laugh at a man who heard the story of the uncle's daughter, the stories of all the others, and spent no time splitting hairs or asking foolish questions, but made his decision at once and packed his bag.

What manner of man? Charles Malcolm could know him a lifetime and never understand.

# Chapter Four

THE sheriff had long ago discarded his sheep-camp habit of rising before the sun, and dozed happily until the ungodly hour of seven-thirty—but not that morning.

"Adolfo," his wife called. "It's Señor Kearney."

"Eh," the sheriff said, "what's the time?"

"Six."

"Oh, it would be him," Montez groaned. "Two days of peace and it starts again!"

He washed and dressed hurriedly, gulped coffee in the kitchen, and greeted his caller in the front room. Kearney was unshaven and smelled strongly of horse, but Montez experienced no fresh alarm until he saw the other caller.

"Rachel!" he said. "Why are you here?"

"I want a safe place for her," Kearney said.

"For Rachel?" Montez asked. "Who would harm her?"

"She was held at Malcolm's ranch," Kearney said. "She'll testify to that."

"Is this true, Rachel?"

"Yes, Sheriff."

"She's afraid to stay at her aunt's," Kearney said. "Can you get a place? I'll pay the board."

"Of course," Montez said. "But——"

"She's going to have a baby," Kearney said, "and another matter we'll go into later."

"So," Montez said softly. "That is different."

Montez could act swiftly when the occasion demanded; within twenty minutes Rachel was installed in his brother's house next door; ten minutes later he was in the courthouse office, reading the paper Kearney presented.

"Bad," he said. "Very bad."

"You have a safe?"

"Yes."

"Keep it there," Kearney said. "And my thanks for understanding, for asking no stupid questions."

"Understanding?" Montez smiled. "I am confused. Do you know what has taken place these past two days?"

"In town?" Kearney said. "No."

"Then listen," Montez said. "Such rumors concerning Señor Malcolm. That he is wanted for murder, robbery, for a dozen crimes, that he has wives and children beyond the achievement of a sultan. That he is preparing to cheat everyone from the archbishop to the banker and disappear, that you will meet him in the plaza for a shoot-out, that—" Montez sighed—"but you see? Now I take all this with a grain of salt. I know my town, and this town loves a little story, it is filled with gossips who can take a chicken bone and blow it into an eagle's wing overnight. But the truth remains—smell some smoke and there's bound to be fire. I would deeply appreciate it if you tell me just what you have in mind?"

"You've guessed," Kearney said. "I'm out to get him, and I've got a fair start."

Montez rubbed his palms on the worn chair arms and nodded soberly. "You have indeed, and you place me in a delicate position. Surely all this will lead to violence."

"He'll start it," Kearney said.

"Granted, but then—?"

"I'll finish it," Kearney said. "And that puts me on the right side, eh?"

"In a sense."

"I'll see it does," he said. "Now excuse me—Malcolm and the others will arrive any time now."

"How fortunate," Montez said. "All the eggs in one basket. . . . Just where were you, Señor Kearney?"

"Seeing the country," he said. "We stopped at Don Roberto's en route."

"Ah," Montez said miserably. "And Don Roberto?"

"Will be in town Saturday."

He left Montez staring blankly at the dirty wall. His footsteps died away; the sheriff came from his chair with a bound. He had two deputies on active duty; it was time to swear in four more, oil the guns, and light the candles. For whom he wasn't sure, but somebody would need a candle before the week was out.

"Carlos!" he called.

"Yes?" Carlos Ramos answered from the county clerk's office across the hallway.

"Get up from your fat ass!" the sheriff roared. "Go get the boys for me . . . pronto!"

Oh, the town was fairly hissing with rumors by one o'clock. Across adobe fences, in the plaza, the bars, everywhere. Kearney and Shaffer had brought a bedraggled Rachel Perez to the sheriff's house at dawn, and Rachel was staying next door and had a suspicious roundness under her dress. At noon Señor Malcolm and Vigil returned, and not far behind them the *bruja* turned her yellow mule into the stable behind her small house. The sheriff had sworn in four additional deputies. A messenger trotted from the bank to Señor Malcolm's house, and Malcolm came downtown for private words with the banker; and from there went directly to the hotel. Word flew around the plaza: he was in the lobby, now he entered the barroom, who was there to listen? Nobody but Wintergreen, Shaffer, and Kearney. Quick, somebody go buy a drink. But the doors were locked and the walls were thick. No one pressed against the doors;

adobe walls stopped all bullets but swinging doors were thin. Better to wait and see . . . ah, someone in there was getting mad.

Malcolm faced Jack Wintergreen across the bar, ignoring Kearney and Shaffer. "I come home," Malcolm said, "and find a hundred malicious lies circulating in my name. I know where they started. I intend to trace them to that source, and bring charges against you, Wintergreen."

"Ought to be fun," Wintergreen said. "Tracing gossip in this town'll take years—you want a drink or are you just killing time?"

"It will take me ten days," Malcolm said, "and I promise you a full slate of charges at the next court session unless you publish a complete retraction."

"Too busy," Wintergreen said.

"You care very little about your business?"

"This?" Wintergreen said. "I just lease the fixtures. Sue and be damned. You can't get blood from a turnip."

"No?" Malcolm said softly.

One short week ago he had the town in his hand; now a bartender laughed in his face and a sheepherder snickered behind his back. The banker had questioned him about wild rumors concerning his plan to milk the town dry and decamp. He felt the rage lifting in his throat and stopped himself only in time; letting go was utter folly. Kearney was sitting at the back table waiting for that precise moment. He was foolish to come charging in here and threaten Wintergreen. He forced his mouth into the dry skeleton of a smile.

"Thought of something?" Wintergreen asked.

"Fortunately, yes."

"Don't tell me," Wintergreen said. "Let me guess—Teresita's goin' to lay a curse on my poor black soul."

Was there nothing Kearney did not know? Malcolm turned from the bar and faced the back corner. He saw Kearney, elbows on the table, and he waited for the man to speak; but Kearney sat, tapping a checker on the board, and the silence stretched wire-taut between them. Again Malcolm brought himself up short. Why was he standing like a dog, bristles up, when Kearney had nothing concrete to use against him?

"My house and ranch are private property," he said. "Signs will be posted to that effect. All trespassers will be shot on sight."

"All?" Kearney asked.

"All!"

"What about you?" Kearney said quietly. "You're a trespasser on this land."

Malcolm marched to the swinging doors, lifted the bar, and passed from sight; and Jack Wintergreen wiped his sweaty face and expelled a whistling gust of breath.

"John, that was close."

"No," Kearney said. "We're just tickling him. Wait till Saturday."

"Just tickling," Shaffer said. "What about that paper Rachel signed?"

"Fleabites," Kearney said. "But you keep biting, pecking away, and maybe all the bites will get so damn painful he'll blow up. He has to do it inside him, not from the fleabites."

"And how do you get inside that man?" Wintergreen asked.

"He'll do that himself," Kearney said. "And while we're waiting on Saturday, you can spread one more rumor, Jack."

"Name it."

"Things are bad along the border," Kearney said. "Villa has got Juarez tangled up, and down the river from there to the Presidio it's tough for a man to get across. Spread a rumor that I've got friends watching every town from Columbus to Presidio just in case a certain person tries to enter Mexico in the near future."

"I can do that," Wintergreen said. "And I savvy why you want him to hear that good news. But you're giving something away there, John. Won't he take heed in case he does pull stakes?"

"You make sure he hears it," Kearney said. "I'll worry about the crossing."

"You reckon he might go south?" Shaffer asked.

"He might," Kearney said. "After Saturday."

He had sent Vigil for Teresita and they sat together in the back room with the big dog rubbing against his leg. He was calmer now, had managed a chuckle at his own ghosts, was able to consider the situation with his old deliberate steadiness. But even as he talked with Teresita, the worry was running thinly in him, like a tooth that ached and subsided and ached again. He had told her everything, as he always did when circumstances warranted, and now he rubbed the dog's neck and gave her time to think.

"That is all?" she asked.

"All he can possibly have," Malcolm said. "Nothing that will cause much damage in court. I can handle that end of it."

"But we do not care about court," Teresita said shrewdly. "For that does not come until spring, and he is present now. Don Roberto will come Saturday, and that is everything."

"Kearney will see him," Malcolm said. "We can't stop him."

"Perhaps," she said. "Now of the girl. Vigil says she signed a paper. We have not seen the paper, but you know what it says?"

"Quite," he said. "Confessing her part in the first night's business."

"But only her part . . . and Vigil's?"

"Yes," he said. "As for Vigil being there, attempting murder, it is her word against his, and nothing directly from me. It will not stand up."

"But you say she will testify that you held her at the ranch against her will?"

"Her word against mine," Malcolm said. "Nothing there."

"But it causes talk," Teresita said. "You must not have idle gossip clouding Don Roberto's mind. I will see to the girl."

So it came to that once more: Teresita would manage the girl. The girl he had taken into his bed for three months and, most likely, brought down with another child. He had no obligations toward Rachel Perez, nor had she the right to assume obligations. She came of her own free will, she had been rewarded; that was the end of the matter. But he had no choice now; the girl must be silenced.

"Well," Teresita said. "You give permission?"

"Very well," he said. "But it must be done before Saturday."

"Two days," Teresita said. "A short time to work."

"Either you can or cannot," he said curtly. "If not, I can manage."

"It will be done," she said. "Now, what of Shaffer and Wintergreen?"

"They are nothing," he said scornfully. "They do not count."

"And Kearney?"

Malcolm rose from the table and walked to the kitchen door. He called, "Vigil!" and faced Teresita as the Indian entered and stood against the wall.

"Watch him," Malcolm said. "From now on, night and day."

"When?" Vigil said.

"Not before Saturday," Malcolm said. "No sooner than mid-afternoon."

"And then?"

"When I give the word," Malcolm said. "And I warn you, Vigil. No more excuses, no more failures."

He watched the Indian leave, saw Teresita to the kitchen door, and returned to his table. He had two days to weave the cut threads together, two days to think of Don Roberto and make his plans. The Martinez family would arrive in late forenoon Saturday, eat dinner at the hotel, and spend the afternoon shopping before they left for home. At one given time during the afternoon he must sit down with Don Roberto and conclude the deal, have all papers ready, get the old fool to the courthouse and make it official. He must do this at one of two times: before Kearney saw Don Roberto, or after. There was chance involved either way, depending on Kearney's approach. It might be wise to talk after, as a good lawyer always desired the last rebuttal; but Kearney was unorthodox, he could not guess how Kearney might present a case. He knew all the arguments Kearney could muster, true, but how would the man phrase those arguments?

And he must consider the daughter seriously, for she was the only member of the family with an ounce of brain. She would be the one who made the final demand, asked the question Don Roberto had ignored for two years: what about an inspection of the mine by outside engineers? Don Roberto had exchanged sheep for gold half a dozen times, gold that came from the mine, yes, but gold taken from the small pocket which was nearly exhausted. One hour's examination by a competent mining engineer would blow everything sky-high. Oh, the gold was there, another five or six thousand dollars worth, but Don Roberto's river land was worth at least fifteen thousand now at the rock bottom price of fifty cents an acre. He had prepared his argument long ago, anticipating Don Roberto's howl of anger when the gold petered out. He would have clear title to the land, he would be utterly shocked to think he had innocently cheated his old friend, therefore he would make up the difference in cash for the land—but he would still own it. Now, with Kearney on the scene, Don Roberto could still go through with the deal, but when the truth came out his previous solution would be worse than useless. But he could not stop now; he had to go on and let the future solve itself.

"Old man," he said, "what would you do?"

The big dog growled and crossed the room and pushed against his leg. They stood together, two misfits, the dog who lived by honest instinct, the man who did not live.

Teresita McKinley began her work that afternoon. She barred her door, drew her curtains, and prepared the curse for Rachel Perez. She could smile when Malcolm made light of her curses, argued that she was exploiting her people, that a curse was all a matter of the mind; but when she began the work, handed down to her from others who had lived in this valley, it became a serious business that seemed to grow of its own volition beneath her fingers and in her heart. She did not know the word "faker" but if she had it would not have mattered. She was forty-two years old, and from her fifteenth year she had known the *poder* and carried on her work. There came a moment, always, when she ceased to think of Malcolm and became herself entirely, as she had been before he came. Then she moved in time-honored pattern, a true *bruja* carrying life and death in her dark face.

She made the curse and carried it in her dress pocket as she walked west along the edge of town, then south through the alleys and lanes to the house of Tony Montez. She knocked and stepped inside smiling as the wife backed away before her. No one refused her entry in this valley. She heard Rachel talking with the children in the back yard, a child herself, already laughing, her stomach full, her fears forgotten. Teresita McKinley saw the clothing on the chest in the corner, the bright green dress too small for the wife of Tony Montez. She slipped her hand into the dress and rubbed her fingers until the powder dissolved and left dull stains within the cloth. Then she turned and faced the wife.

"She will wear that dress tonight," Teresita said. "Such a beautiful dress. Fit for a wedding—or a funeral!"

She passed from the house and walked slowly up Ranchitos Road. She feared no one in the house. No one would touch the dress or tell the girl, and the girl would wear it tonight when she promenaded in the plaza, secure with the sheriff and Kearney protecting her. But when Rachel Perez returned from the plaza and sat in the kitchen, eating cookies, drinking frothy chocolate, someone would say the words and it would start. No need to warn Rachel Perez against testifying in court. She would not open her mouth if they tortured her with fire. She would sicken from tonight onward and, if the curse was not removed, she would die as surely as the *bruja* walked proudly in the brown dust, in the evening shadows stealing over the town.

"Now you," Teresita McKinley said fiercely. "Now you, Carlitos!"

All day Friday Kearney knew he was watched. He remained in the barroom until late afternoon, crossed to the general store, left by the back door, and walked swiftly down the back road past Guadalupe Church toward the ridge. He ducked behind a wall, ran to the south end, and saw Vigil slipping along the houses on the north side of the road. Kearney retraced his steps and waited until Vigil came abreast before he stepped into the road. The Indian did not stop. He met Kearney's gaze, bobbed his head like a turtle, and continued up the road.

"Vigil!" Kearney said.

"Yes."

"I'm going back to the hotel," he said. "Save your feet."

Vigil returned and stopped beside him; and for a moment Kearney caught emotion in that flat, unwrinkled face. The fleeting anger and hatred was expected, but shame was beginning to break the mask. Vigil was a proud man, a man who could not be smashed into the dirt; what had been a job was now a matter of honor.

"Will you walk with me?" Kearney said. "On such a pleasant day."

Vigil grunted and swung into stride with him, up the road, past Guadalupe Church, through the dark alley between the store and harness shop where the doctor's Model T stood, the only car in town, black and tinny, alien in this world.

"I'll be here tonight," Kearney said. "In the same room. Don't try it tonight, Vigil."

Eyes were watching them and Vigil knew he was drawn into a foolish position. He would not speak, he hated to walk away the loser in this game, but he edged toward the porch shadows outside the courthouse.

"Vigil," Kearney said. "Tomorrow is Saturday. I won't leave town. But Sunday I'm riding north. Questa, Red River Canyon. Where is your mine, Vigil?"

Someone laughed coarsely in the group of men loafing before the courthouse doors. Vigil walked faster on the hard-packed earth, moccasins scuffing softly. Watching him go, Kearney wondered what Malcolm would say to the news. Not that it mattered. He had another card to play tomorrow and, granted that Malcolm might counter all the known elements when they met Don Roberto, he had worked last night and this morning with pen and paper to create the unexpected. Wintergreen had approved it, Shaffer had rocked with glee.

"Good afternoon, Señor Kearney."

"Sheriff," he said. "How are you?"

"Sad."

"Because of me?"

"I've been looking for you," Montez said. "Teresita came to my brother's house late yesterday. She placed a curse in Rachel's green dress, the girl wore it last night, and my brother's wife let it slip at bedtime. They are striking back at you, Señor Kearney, through an innocent girl. Do you know how my people are when the *bruja* puts the curse on them?"

"They die," he said, "unless someone buys the *bruja* off."

"Yes," Montez said, "and do not make light of the curse. It is already working on Rachel. She will never testify now, she will deny the confession she signed. That is nothing, you understand, weighed against the girl's life. She is caught, and it is not her fault."

"You are trying to say that no one can buy this *bruja* off?"

"There is one," Montez said.

"Me."

"No one but you," Montez said. "And I fear for the girl, knowing you."

"Then you do not know me," he said. "How long will it take for Rachel—this time I mean, this particular curse?"

"Two weeks," Montez said. "A month at most."

"Then tomorrow and Sunday will not hurt her too badly?"

"I am familiar with this business," Montez said. "The first week for most is like slow poison. The second week it spreads like fire."

"I'll do something about it," Kearney said. "You have my promise."

"To buy the *bruja* off?"

"No," he said roughly. "You know me, you say, then you know I'd pay no *bruja* a plugged cent."

"And you wonder why I am sad?"

"Sheriff," Kearney said, "I have my affairs, you have yours. Let me say one thing—keep that confession in your safe."

He walked away into the sun glare, away from the blank-faced man, across the plaza, into the coolness of the barroom, knowing what the sheriff was thinking and disliking that part of it most of all.

"Beer?" Wintergreen said.

"Whisky," he said, "and no palaver."

Oh, things were really happening now. Rachel Perez had the curse on her and opinion was divided in that respect: some swore it was Malcolm protesting his too potent virility, some swore it was more of the business they did not understand. The witch would be flying tonight on her broomstick, and everyone drew the curtains and spoke in soft tones. Something must happen very soon, and other rumors had begun during the day concerning Don Roberto Martinez and Malcom; and yet another, very sly, repeated only in the *cantina* at the foot of the slope below the plaza, that Señora Maria Martinez was very young, Don Roberto was getting old, and Malcolm rode the Tres Piedras trail too often for business alone.

Saturday was the busy day in Taos. Word had spread down Ranchitos and south to Ranchos, northwest to Arroyo Seco and Arroyo Hondo, to Cordova and even to the pueblo. Everyone came to town on Saturday, to buy supplies and visit, to dance at night and get drunk, to ride home happily through the night. By ten o'clock the plaza was crowded, not another wagon or horse could be jammed against the posts and rails; at eleven o'clock Don Roberto Martinez came riding off the river road astride his fine bay mare, his sons riding with him, his wife in the fancy new buggy driven by José, Isidro's wife and children and Flavia in the old two-seater buggy made for growing families. They pulled into the livery barn, tossed the reins to the hostlers as befitted their station, walked leisurely to the plaza where they greeted friends and neighbors as Don Roberto led his family into the hotel lobby and his daughter went straight to the general store with the ranch order. Don Roberto bought his sons their first drink in the barroom, excused himself to visit the bank and stop in on his daughter's buying, and returned to the lobby where his wife was the center of a growing court on the large back couch, a court composed of older women, a few foolish girls, and several young men who had evidently forgotten their manners. The sheriff was conspicuous by his absence but his deputies were in evidence. Carlos was in the lobby, Pedro in the barroom, the four temporaries scattered outside.

The Sheriff was on the courthouse roof, seated behind the fire wall with a double-barreled shotgun. His youngest son was in the alley facing Pueblo Road. When Charles Malcolm swung from his front gate, that son whistled. The oldest son was behind the courthouse. He heard that whistle, thrust his thumb and forefinger in his mouth, and whistled twice. The sheriff nodded to himself and inched closer to the drain; and then his brother's boy, to the west on the harness shop roof, gave another whistle. Vigil was over there on the west side in the vicinity of Guadalupe Church. The sheriff laid the shotgun across his knees and dried his palms. Now let it come, if it was coming today. He could do no more.

Charles Malcolm entered the lobby and went directly to the large group surrounding Don Roberto. He was delayed in breaking through the circle and took advantage of this opportunity to shake hands with Isidro, greet his wife, find Miguel's hand, and note with relief that Flavia was absent. Then Don Roberto called, "Hey, Carlitos," and gave him a big embrace twice over.

"Will you eat with us?" Don Roberto asked.

"Delighted," Malcolm said. "Doña Maria, you took the ride well?"

"Very well, señor," Maria Martinez said softly. "It is good to see you."

Then Don Roberto was leading them all into the dining room where two tables in the rear were joined to serve them. Malcolm sat on his right, Isidro and Miguel across the board, and others down the line to Maria at the foot. Times had changed a good deal in the past ten years; now a man allowed his wife to eat with him in town. It was a good sign, or a foolish one, depending on the woman. Malcolm privately believed it a stupid move, especially when Flavia arrived and quietly took the vacant chair beside Miguel. She acknowledged his greeting, spoke politely in return, and bent over her plate. She never ceased to worry him, the way she lived within that mousy exterior, yet met a man on equal terms of intelligence and refused to bow down to any man. He could not guess her thoughts, and he felt the strength in her, the kind of courage and strength that made the real women of this country, the matriarchs who weighed no more than thistledown yet ruled empires with soft words and gentle wishes. Malcolm talked and ate, the table cleared, the coffee cups were filled, and Don Roberto cleared his throat importantly.

"Now, Carlitos. You wish to speak?"

He had delayed any fast routine until he was greeted. He took his cue from the manner in which Don Roberto met him today. If the greeting had been cool, he planned to wait until Kearney spoke his piece. If Don Roberto was cheerful, then he wanted to grasp the hot iron.

"If I may," he said. "Shall we speak alone?"

"No," Don Roberto said expansively. "Isidro, Miguel, Flavia—we've kicked it up and down together." Then he looked along the table meaningfully and held his tongue until the others, led by Maria, rose and entered the lobby. "Now," Don Roberto said, "let us talk."

"Perhaps there's no need for me to speak," Malcolm said. "If you have reached a decision."

"We have not," Don Roberto said. "Not all together yet."

He made himself smile. "And who doubts me?"

"One guess, Carlitos."

He smiled at Miguel, at Flavia. "It would be you, Flavia, and you, Miguel. I respect your caution. What doubts do you voice?"

Miguel Martinez had ridden in to the ranch from the north camp at dawn, bathed in the spring, changed clothes, and cinched his saddle on a fresh horse. He still smelled of sheep and his dark face was darker here in town, contrasted against the blue walls of the dining room. Miguel shrugged and nodded to his sister.

"She'll talk for me," he said. "We're one, me and the kid."

"Flavia," Malcolm said. "Will you tell me why you do not think this transaction is good? Why it is not fair in every way to all, will profit all?"

"Father?" Flavia said.

"Go on," Don Roberto said resignedly.

"Thank you, Father," Flavia said. "Señor Malcolm, I am sorry but I do not think of profit. I only think of the land. We never sell our land. We have always kept it. Why should we change from what was good to what no one can foresee when we do not need profit?"

He had carefully reviewed every argument last night, every rebuttal, every possibility, and being the man he was, he discarded every one in that moment. He drew the papers from his coat pocket, the fresh white papers completely drawn up and filled in but for signatures, and tossed them carelessly before Don Roberto.

"Then I can say nothing," Malcolm said gently. "We have discussed this for two years. We know the value of the land, we know what you will receive from the mine each year, we know how I will use the land. Don Roberto, if this is your daughter's wish, I bow to it. I will not trouble you again."

He pushed his chair away and laid his napkin beside his cup. He smiled at them all, nodded soberly to Don Roberto, and rose from the table; and it all hung on this instant, everything he had learned about these people, everything in them that existed in the present, yet carried long roots of tradition from the past. Daughters were wonderful pieces of humanity to these people, valuable in the house, valuable to marry and bring other families into one larger, stronger family, with more strength and cohesiveness for all; but daughters had never sat at the council table. There were exceptions, yes, but when the last hand was dealt, then the *patrón* must count his beads one last time if he was a man. For if he divided his authority, he would never reclaim it. Charles Malcolm rose from the table and Don Roberto Martinez said,

"Wait . . . sit down, Carlitos."

"To talk?" Malcolm smiled. "Yes, with pleasure. But no more business, eh?"

"Sit down," Don Roberto said flatly. "Sit down, we will talk business. . . . I accept your proposition."

He saw the girl's face as she turned her head from her father. Miguel snorted and looked down at his coffee cup. A father had just lost two children and felt no pain; but what was a little pain compared to gold? Charles Malcolm walked to the sideboard, brought the pen and ink bottle to the table, and seated himself beside Don Roberto.

"Everything is here," he said. "You understand when I say I do not wish to go through this again, neither for myself or for you, old friend. Let us sign these papers, go to the courthouse, transact the business there, and shake hands."

"The pen," Don Roberto said gruffly.

"Malcolm!" John Kearney called from the barroom door. "Ho, Malcolm . . . there you are."

Don Roberto paused, smiling in recognition, as Kearney crossed the room and stood at his side and dropped one hand on Malcolm's arm.

"Señor Kearney," Don Roberto said. "It is good to see you."

"Good to see all of you," Kearney said thickly, and Malcolm smelled the brandy on his breath and knew the man was no drunker than himself but playing a role, and giving him no chance to intrude. "Sorry to bust in," Kearney said. "Been looking all over for you, Malcolm. I'm riding out to inspect some more land this afternoon so I got everything lined up for us like we agreed."

Charles Malcolm tried to rise and the fingers clamped on his shoulder like a vise and held him helpless against his chair seat. Kearney pulled a sheaf of papers from his right coat pocket and sorted them into two piles directly under Don Roberto's nose. He repocketed one pile and pushed the other beside Malcolm's cup.

"I got everything down like you wanted," Kearney said. "Here's my written agreement to deliver five hundred cows and twenty of my top bulls to you on or before March first, via El Paso, Albuquerque, Santa Fe, and wherever the hell your nearest station is up here. Price like we settled last night, to be counted off the cars. Here's the other paper you wanted, that agreement from the boys I'm repping for down there to deliver two thousand head of the same in June. You can look 'em over, but it's like we agreed on. Now I better get to riding, but I'll see you tomorrow before I leave . . . sorry to butt in, Don Roberto. Adios."

He stepped back and swung around behind Malcolm, and the girl was watching him with a strange, unbelieving stare, and the boy beside her, that had to be the other brother, was looking at him, then at Malcolm, and clenching his big fists on the table. He staggered just right, hit an empty chair, wove his way through the door into the barroom, and, once around the corner, took his gun belt and Colt from Ed Shaffer, buckled it on, and stepped against the wall facing the bar where Wintergreen served a capacity Saturday crowd and watched him over those bent heads. He could not hear talk from the dining room, but Shaffer slipped over and watched through the door behind the protective, moving cover of a dozen men. He could not see those faces in the dining room, or hear them, but Shaffer was grinning suddenly and he could guess the words.

For Don Roberto Martinez was staring woodenly at the papers on the corner of the table, and Charles Malcolm was staring at those papers, searching helplessly for words. The girl spoke first, her voice soft and stern.

"For sheep, yes? Never for cows across the river, no! You would sign papers, you would post a bond! Father, you hear!"

"Cattle," Miguel Martinez said. "Cattle on *our* land! Five hundred in the spring, two thousand in the summer. That many on thirty thousand acres, where it takes fifty acres for a cow? *Patrón,* you hear!"

Don Roberto Martinez had the pen in his right hand, point poised over the ink bottle. He looked at the pen and threw it suddenly, away from him to the floor behind the table. He looked at Charles Malcolm and the bewilderment softened into sadness, and then, as only a small man could, the sadness hardened into anger that turned his face fiery red and lifted the pulsing veins above his temples. He snatched the clean white papers in both hands, ripped them apart, threw them to the floor.

"Why do I sit here?" Don Roberto said hoarsely. "Flavia, get your mother. We are going home!"

He rose so abruptly that his chair clattered backward to the floor, and the others were up as swiftly, Flavia and Miguel almost smiling, Isidro still looking stupidly at the torn papers and the ink bottle, upset, spreading its black embonpoint across the white cloth. Don Roberto walked—strode proudly was the word—to the lobby door, looking neither right nor left, leading his family into the lobby, collecting his wife, going on through the lobby to the street. Behind him, Flavia touched her brother's arm.

"Please get her," she said.

"*¿Por qué?*"

"I'll see you at the stable," she said, and was gone, back through the lobby and out the rear door into the hallway.

Malcolm did not move until the ink came dripping over the table edge and threatened his gray trousers. Then he moved over deliberately and signaled the waitress. He bent down and gathered the torn papers, and held Kearney's forgeries in his hands. The girl poured fresh, hot coffee and he drank without taste, she poured again, left the pot, and went away. He laughed softly, for he could not trust himself to rise and leave the dining room just yet. Considering everything, he thought dully, he hadn't missed a single point! Brought it to a successful conclusion, pen in hand, ink ready, the culmination of two long years—two years of listening to foolish talk, of taking desperate chances with a woman he wanted even more desperately as the final act in his plan. Two years of that, and wiped out in one minute by a man he had known one week.

"Kearney," he said aloud. "Kearney!"

The boy from the kitchen came to Kearney and pulled timidly at his sleeve.

"Please, señor," the boy said, "come with me."

"Where, *chico?*"

Shaffer was beside him, tugging at his other arm, grinning so broadly the leathery skin threatened to split.

"In back, señor," the boy said. "Hurry, please."

"It's off," Shaffer said. "Threw the pen, spilled the ink, walked out."

"Where is he?" Kearney asked.

"Still there," Shaffer said. "Can't move, I guess. Been hit like a poleaxed steer."

"Señor?"

"Who is it?" he asked, bending down, looking closer at the boy. "A man?"

"No, señor. A lady."

He said, "Watch Malcolm, Ed," and headed for the back door that led through the storeroom to the alley, pulling the boy along so rapidly those short legs barely touched the floor. He reached the alley door, dropped a dollar into the boy's hand, and touched the suddenly frightened face with one finger. "Run along," he said, "and tell this to no one, hear?"

"I hear, señor."

He ducked outside and found her waiting beside a stack of empty beer barrels. He removed his hat and drew her behind the stack where they faced down the slope toward the spring and the livery stable and all the valley flowing away over the rolling hills toward Ranchos; and the first words she spoke were:

"You were not drunk."

"No," he said. "But you guessed that. So did your brother. You shouldn't be here."

"I would be no other place," she said. "Nor would Miguel if he dared. Those papers—were they worth the ink?"

"No," Kearney said. "But worth the time."

"How can I thank you?" she said. "For me, for my brother, for my father when he is calm and can think. ... Why, why did you do it?"

"I lied to your father the other day," Kearney said. "But it was a harmless lie. I had no choice. It was necessary."

"But why?"

"Look," he said. "You'd better go. I could stop at your place Monday afternoon."

"Oh, no," she said. "It would not be correct."

"Then where can we talk?"

"Well," she said wonderingly, "well ... do you know Señor Shaffer's?"

"Yes."

"Below him across the river," she said. "The springs are there. But——"

"Bring your brother," he said. "I want to know him. He's a good man."

"As is the other," she said quickly. "When he thinks."

Then she was gone, running down the slope like a deer, surprising him with the sudden emergence of that youthfulness; and as suddenly, reaching Santa Fe Road, slowing to a brisk but ladylike walk. He watched her go and thought, "She asked no foolish questions, nothing; she understood the moment it happened back there."

He had never met another like her. He had to see her again.

# Chapter Five

THE actors had departed their stage but people clung hopefully to the plaza like moths in the flame's singe, watching the hotel doors, glancing toward Pueblo Road. Don Roberto had led his family from town, his face blacker than night. Malcolm had gone straight home, and Kearney had not appeared since those dangerous moments in the dining room. But the people watched, for this was better than a bullfight, and the sheriff held another meeting with his deputies.

"Vigil has gone to the house," Montez said. "You watch there, Pedro. Carlos stays here. You two, behind the inn. You two, west and east sides of the plaza."

"For how long?" Carlos asked.

"Until I give the word."

"And if nothing happens?"

"I pray for that," Montez said shortly. "In the meanwhile, assist the Virgin with your better efforts."

"What is all this?" Carlos said. "I don't know what we're doing, Adolfo."

"I do," Montez said. "That is sufficient. Eat your supper, take your posts."

"And you?"

"I'll be near."

Montez watched them go and sighed in momentary relief. He could go home for supper, look in on Rachel, and saddle his best horse. He wanted instant mobility tonight, tomorrow, every day until this business ended; and he wanted no bloodshed in his town. He clucked his tongue in wonder at Kearney, who was creating more trouble than the plague. What would the man do next?

Charles Malcolm was pondering that same question. Vigil sat on the wall bench, cleaning his Winchester, curling his toes into the floor cracks. Teresita had come soon after he returned, taken his measure, and busied herself over the stove; and he had downed one long drink, studied the bottle thoughtfully, and pushed it aside. He sat three hours in silence while Teresita stayed ostensibly busy in the kitchen and Vigil cleaned, oiled, and recleaned his Winchester, an eternal movement of greasy fingers that had surely worn several thousandth inches of metal from the shining mechanism.

Watching those fingers gave Malcolm a focus for his thoughts, steadied him as a metronome brought cadence to a scale, leveled his anger and restored sane judgment. He knew how Teresita was thinking: she had watched the miracle of a man's face as it plummeted into despair, struck rock-bottom, and began the desperate finger-clawing climb to hope. But she had seen—as he felt himself—the slowness in that climb alien to all she knew of him. He had suffered reverses in the past and rebounded swiftly with fresh schemes that brought greater victories; but tonight she smelled defeat, decay, within the man where, in the past, no emotion betrayed his inner thoughts. Now supper was ready, evening darkness falling, and she came from the kitchen with her inner excitement showing in her hands and body movement. She was closer to her triumph over him than ever before . . . or so she thought. She had guessed correctly his inward turmoil, his early feeling of utter defeat, but she was never further from capturing his mind and body. For he had thought it all out while he sat through the afternoon's shank, and now he would play the most dangerous game of his life: one against them all.

"Supper?" she said.

"Thank you, no," he said politely.

"But you must eat, Carlitos."

"Not tonight."

"Ah, poor man!"

She probed so gently, searching into his mind. Something had gone out of him at last, part of the steel that made him different from all men in her eyes. He had played a game with his own rules governing every turn of the cards, and Kearney had whipped him into the dirt. So at last, she was thinking, he needed more from her than *bruja* curses and shrewd advice.

"Does it matter so much?" she said. "A little land, a few more sheep?"

Did it matter? He had watched the work of six years dissolve in one moment, and wasted no tears over lost profit. It was never the profit that counted; it was the feeling, almost of exaltation, that he knew when he mastered circumstances and people. And all that was gone, or going, as he sat in the big room. Don Roberto was a power among his people, and everyone would know how Señor Malcolm tried to upset an old order of life, tried to cheat a friend; and once they knew the lie that was now truth, he lost his greatest asset: their confidence in him. He could no longer do business with these people. If a man needed money and no one would make the loan, would he come to Señor Malcolm? No, he would starve first. When court rolled around would Señor Malcolm have a crowded docket, defending these people against gringos and outlanders? No, and those cases already set for spring would slip from him during the winter. Would they come to him when the *bruja* placed a curse and beg his help? No, they would die first. And most of all, when Don Roberto died, an event already planned for the near future but impossible now, would his widow marry Señor Malcolm and bring to him more of that land across the river? No, not if she wished it herself even after today; for she would die, too, and not by her hand or his.

Did it matter? A little land, a few more sheep? No, not in that way. What hurt, what cut deeply, was the unforgettable truth that he was finished forever in this valley. If he stayed on, as he could, he would become a hanger-on, a small, shoddy part of the past, subject to laughter. If Teresita had her way he would become a slave to her in mind and body. He had thought it all through and now he must play the game to the only possible end, using her, using Vigil, until it was time to go. And when he left, he went alone. You never went back. You shook off the past and went on toward the future that always shone brighter.

"Carlitos," she said, "does it matter so much?"

"No," he said.

"But Kearney does?"

"Yes," he said. "Or don't you agree?"

"I agree," she said. "For what he has done—give him his reward."

"Vigil," Malcolm said, "Kearney told you he would visit our mine tomorrow?"

"Yes, *patrón*."

"Leave tonight," Malcolm said. "Greet him tomorrow. On the road, in the canyon—choose your place."

"*Gracias, patrón*."

Malcolm sat quietly until the Indian ate and left the house. He heard the horse walk from the stable and pass on into the night; and then he managed a smile.

"Do I smell food?"

"Oh yes," Teresita said. "Ready an hour."

"Now I'm hungry," he said. "You see how lucky I am."

"How so?"

"I have Vigil," he said. "I have Oso—" he rubbed the big dog roughly—"and I have you."

"You will always have me," she said.

She set the table, brought the food, and while they ate she spoke of Rachel and how the curse was working and did he wish her to leave it on.

"She will not come to you now," Teresita said. "And you know how it will end if no one comes."

"Leave it for now," he said. "We'll teach them a lesson."

"Let her suffer a little, scare them all?" she smiled. "You are yourself again, Carlitos."

"And you?"

"Ready to serve you," she said softly. "In any way."

He moved deliberately into the trap of her words, not too swiftly, but enough to give her lasting hope. He finished his meal and showed his fatigue, rubbing his eyes, leaning heavily over his plate.

"It is late," he said. "I am very tired, Teresita."

"You wish me to go?"

"It would be best," he said. "Tonight."

She could transform herself when she smiled in a certain way; it was a strange experience to watch the pitted face acquire a fleeting beauty all its own. That beauty flashed as she touched his shoulder and left the house.

Malcolm sat a minute, mixed a hot drink, took the lamp, and retired to his small bedroom. He drank slowly, watching the lamp flame, knowing she was watching from the darkness. He undressed, smothered the lamp, and changed into his riding clothes. He laid out the heavy rifle, the field glasses, then lay back and closed his mind to all thought until two o'clock.

At that time he turned the big dog into the yard, saddled the gray mare, and led her through the front gate and west across the fields toward the Questa Road. He would be on the highest ridge above the river tomorrow afternoon. Kearney was bound to come that way, and he would be waiting. Vigil could never trap the man; it would be a game of tag until Kearney came riding wide on his return from the mine; and then Malcolm would have his chance. He laid his hand on the rifle stock in the saddle boot and mounted the gray mare.

Kearney took Ed Shaffer upstairs after supper, opened his window wide, and gave his orders for the night.

"You sleep first. I'll watch till ten, then you can stand until Jack locks up at twelve. He'll roust us out."

"What time?"

"Four," Kearney said. "And don't forget the rifle."

"Right."

"I want to be five miles north by five o'clock," he said.

"Slave driver."

"Bell goat," he laughed.

Ed Shaffer went down the hall to catch a few hours' sleep. Kearney made himself comfortable on the sagging bed, socked feet on the chair, Colt on the pillow. He laid out three cigars, got the first one burning evenly, and began the long watch. He thought of Vigil, who would certainly be waiting along the road tomorrow, and Malcolm, who might take advantage of the situation. He smoked through the passage of time until the boy came up from the barroom and woke Shaffer. When Shaffer tapped on his door he said, "A minute," and dressed completely, opened his Gladstone, and removed two articles wrapped in a shirt. He let Shaffer in, took a last look into the plaza, and went down the hall to Shaffer's room. He did not wake until Wintergreen called softly, "Time to go, John," and then he was moving sleepily with Shaffer, following Wintergreen downstairs, through the drafty rear hall, into the yard where horses stood, blanket rolls and gun boots in place.

"Got a good one for you," Wintergreen said.

Kearney drew the .94 from the boot and checked the balance. The saddle gun lay solid and familiar across his left palm, steel brother to the thousands used across the land. He felt the rectangular lump of two cartridge boxes tied in the blanket roll, thumbed the rear sight for setting, and slid the .94 back into the boot.

"Used much?" he asked.

"Just enough," Wintergreen said. "Abraham says it shoots a little low to the left at three hundred."

"Right," he said. "Ready, Ed?"

"Ready."

"See you Monday, Jack," he said. "Keep the home fires burning."

He mounted, pressed the brown horse between his legs, and trailed Shaffer to the west down Ranchitos Road, then north around town to the Questa Road and across that well-defined trail toward Arroyo Hondo and the talus ridges running toward the gorge. They crossed the deep arroyo, quartered northwesterly through the timber, and rode onto the Questa Road again at dawn. They lay close against the heavy bulk of the main range, rode San Cristobal valley, and broke onto the high ridge overlooking Questa valley at ten o'clock of a clear, bright October day.

"Better stick to the trees," Shaffer said. "Easiest route to the canyon."

"We're not going up the canyon," he said.

"No?"

"Waste of time," Kearney said. "It won't matter now if he's got bonanza or borrasca. Let's rest."

They tied the horses and stretched out beneath the trees and looked down upon the valley floor while the sun climbed toward zenith and all of Sunday ran a leisurely course in the village and surrounding farms. People down there had attended Mass and were coming home, in wagons, horseback, walking in small groups beside the river; chimneys smoked as Sunday dinner went on the stove, children played around the yards and haystacks, rode ponies on the meadows. At twelve o'clock by Shaffer's repeater, Kearney unwrapped his package.

"Now what the hell," Shaffer said. "I know what glasses are, but why the mirrors."

Kearney cradled the telescoped spyglass across his legs and polished the lenses. He opened the glass, sighted on the village, and focused in until the houses leaped clearly into view.

"Try it," he said.

He smoked while Shaffer fiddled with the glass, sighted on the church cross, on barns, on a boy switching his pony toward the river.

"Works fine," Shaffer said. "Brings 'em right into your hand."

"Sure you can work it?"

"Easy."

"Collapse it," he said. "You'll use it today."

He held one of the small, round mirrors in his left hand, blew on the glass, and polished the bright surface. The mirror was brass-backed, five inches in diameter, minus handle or wall hook. Kearney moved into the shadows, cupped the mirror in his hand, and held it facing the sun.

"Comes from the old signal system Miles used against the Apaches," he said. "Hold it this way, canted away from the direct sun glare, then flip it so it reflects, count three, flip it away. Better carry it in your jacket pocket."

"Now what am I supposed to be," Shaffer smiled. "General Miles or some barebutt Apache?"

"A little of both," Kearney said. "I'll ride down to the river, then move along this side of the Red toward the Rio. You stay up on the high ridges and trail me. Follow me with the glass, watch for Vigil and Malcolm. Ed, all this depends on you. I'll stop and give you a look every few minutes. You can see me in the glass. When I look, if it's clear, give me two flashes. If you spot one or both of them, give me three flashes. And watch for the same signal from me after you finish. I'll keep working toward the river, then downstream to Cedar Springs. Stay above me all the way . . . all right?"

"You're riding wide open," Shaffer said. "Vigil is one helluva shot."

"I'm better," he said quietly. "I'll take the chance."

"And if we see 'em?"

"Don't shoot to hit until you have to," Kearney said.

He mounted the brown horse and swung down the long slope, riding through the thinning trees onto the fading green mat of frost-nipped grass, to the river bank opposite Malcolm's ranch yard. He turned downstream and began his ride, following the river until the walls rose up and formed the impassable gorge. He climbed to the ridgetop, dipped into the next canyon, climbed again, moving steadily. He stopped on a bald knob, looked far up where timber was blue-black, and saw the two quick flashes of sunlight reflected from Shaffer's mirror.

"Good man," he said.

He rode slowly, saving the horse, the .94 pressing solidly against his right thigh. He began sweating as the sun arced west and shone brightly into his face. He rode against the pull of gravity and the horse's shifting, moving body, looking up regularly and, always, catching the two quick flashes of sunlight. He had expected no trouble at this time of day. If Vigil spotted him, which was almost certain, Vigil would anticipate his route and ride ahead to set the trap at Cedar Springs. Kearney knew nothing of the springs but, from the nature of the country, a deeper side canyon would thrust downward at that point into the Rio Grande; and there was the ideal situation for Vigil. He rode on to the entrance of the Red into the Rio, pulled back from the dark, flat shadow of the main gorge, and glanced upward more often as he closed on Cedar Springs. Mounting a high cross ridge, he saw the mirror flashes far above in the timber—two, and then the third flash.

"Chicken in the pot," he said.

Kearney rode off the ridge into the canyon bottom, turned the brown horse west, and picked his way among the house-sized boulders. He saw a fault and followed it upward to the next ridge, into a thin stand of timber, and found the deeper canyon at his feet, cutting downward toward the river, opening in its serpentine course to form a cove beach on the water. A man riding that canyon to the main gorge would be in full view of anyone on the south side, in those ledges and rimrocks. Kearney chose his route and sent the brown horse down; and halfway to the canyon floor entered trees growing thickly for a distance of fifty yards or so. Entering that stand, he drew the .94, dismounted, and tied the horse. He ran through the trees until he found his spot, an upthrust arm of rock, weathered and ragged, giving him cover and a good view of the south rim. He crawled from the trees to that rock and up the inner flank until he squirmed into a crevice and peered between rocks and saw the south rim of the canyon far above. He dug his elbows in beneath the .94 and then he began searching that rim, rock by rock, rubble by rubble, from the east on down toward the main gorge.

Vigil had waited along the Questa Road through the night and into the morning, until he knew Kearney had by passed the road; then he waited patiently for Kearney to return and pick up his man far down the sloping ridges above the Rio gorge. Vigil rode the curve of a bow until he reached the south rim of Cedar Springs canyon. He left his horse down the slope and ran silently through the scrub timber and took a position on a pinnacle overlooking the canyon. Kearney had to cross here, where Vigil knew all the ground like the palm of his hand, and when he did he would be exposed in the canyon bottom. Vigil eased his Winchester forward and began his silent watch. He saw Kearney leave the timber on the north rim and put his horse to a fault trail. Kearney disappeared into a stand of trees and Vigil waited for his man to reappear lower down in easier range. Vigil had the patience but the time clock in his head suddenly exploded warning when horse and rider failed to appear. Directly opposite him and just below the patch of timber, an upthrust pile of rock formed cover for a dozen horses; and Vigil had no time to duck when the slug struck rock beside his head and ricocheted into the sky, followed by the sharp, flat report of the .94. Vigil flung himself backward. Kearney had not missed, had shot exactly where he intended. That was another insult to Vigil's pride. He crept along the rim and edged forward to a fresh position.

Charles Malcolm was out of his element in the open country, understood the fact, and acted accordingly. He took up a position above Cedar Springs canyon where he could watch the Questa Road, the canyon, and the country to the south. He passed an uncomfortable morning, striding back and forth in the trees, slapping his arms, eating his lunch in mid-morning when hunger opened a hole in his stomach. At three in the afternoon he was losing patience. He used his field glasses for the twentieth time, having no hope, and saw it all unfold below: Kearney threading through the trees toward the canyon while, hidden from Kearney's sight, Vigil suddenly appeared and circled to the south side of the canyon. Malcolm ran to his horse, drew the rifle from the boot, and ran down the long ridge to a commanding position. Keeping to cover, Malcolm descended five hundred yards to that point at which the ridge fell away abruptly toward Cedar Springs canyon. He was three hundred yards from Vigil when he wormed his way to a nest of rock and unshipped his glasses; and he watched Kearney approach the north rim and estimated that range as approximately four hundred and twenty-five yards. Malcolm made his sight adjustments, settled the rifle on a hump of grass, and laid his glasses aside. Watching closely, he saw Vigil crawl into position, saw Kearney vanish in the trees halfway down the north canyon wall, heard the shot and saw Vigil jerk back in surprise. Vigil changed positions and crept to the rim; and Malcolm cocked the heavy Ballard and settled into firing position, breathing slowly, calming his nerves.

Vigil fired, the .45-.70 report came up dull and heavy. Then Kearney shot and Vigil drew back, crawled to the west, and edged forward again. The pattern formed as if Malcolm had drawn up a precise military exercise, knowing how it would go and how it must end. Kearney was behind that thick spire of rock. When Kearney moved, up or down, he was exposed. Malcolm snuggled the Ballard against his cheek and waited. He saw Vigil's horse cropping grass on the back slope and he was entirely unprepared for the shock when a rifle crashed to the south and Vigil's horse dropped.

For Ed Shaffer had used his spy glass, made his own wide circle to the south and back to the northwest, and Vigil was afoot and Malcolm was no longer the invisible man. He could not see the rifleman to the south but it was Shaffer or Wintergreen—and most likely the sheepman.

Then Vigil was sliding back from the rim, running crablike for the trees, and the unseen rifleman kicked dust behind Vigil. Vigil reached the trees and vanished, and Malcolm saw Kearney trotting up the slope toward the patch of timber on the north side of the canyon. Charles Malcolm swung the Ballard, brought Kearney's shoulders into his sight ring, took up trigger slack; and someone whistled just behind him. He turned on one elbow and saw the sheriff, astride his great black horse, rifle across the saddle horn, muzzle centered almost negligently on Malcolm.

"No," the sheriff said gently. "Please lay your rifle beside you, Señor Malcolm."

Malcolm lowered the hammer and rose unsteadily, half-numb with shock. He held the Ballard as he walked toward the sheriff, refusing to put it aside, clinging stubbornly to that much concrete evidence of sanity.

"Well," he said harshly. "Well?"

"You are foolish to ride today," Montez said. "You are more of the town, no? Let us say we never met. You ride for home, I will go my way."

Malcolm thought of Vigil but he did not hesitate. He went around the black horse and walked stiff-legged up the ridge toward the trees, clinging to his last shred of control. He untied the mare and rode eastward for the main road, and heard shots from the canyon. He had failed Vigil as the Indian had never failed him, and in doing so he had failed himself. He remembered long-forgotten words, read or heard, that a man had to enter the caves of fear to find true courage. The sheriff had turned him from the final cave and spoken the rule that would govern all action thereafter: that he was fair game, that Kearney had the sanction of the law.

When Shaffer fired from the south, Kearney saw the arm movement as Vigil leaped back from the rim. Sliding down from his perch, running for his horse, Kearney glanced up canyon, saw one man rising to his feet and another on a black horse, and took it all in with that fleeting look. He laughed as he swung the brown horse, mounted, and descended the fault trail in a rush, crossed the canyon floor, and tackled the south wall. The horse found a path and they went scrambling up over the rim into a jumble of rock and juniper. He spotted the dead horse, heard Shaffer's strident whistle, and saw Vigil. The Indian ran south and west, leaping rocks, winding through trees, disappearing at last in the first of the rough benches above the gorge. Vigil would not track him again today. Kearney trotted forward and met Ed Shaffer beside the dead horse. Malcolm had vanished, Montez was no longer in sight.

"An awful temptation," Shaffer said. "I had him cold, John. Did I do right?"

"You'll never do better," Kearney said. "But you missed something."

"Malcolm?" Shaffer said. "I never missed him. I saw him laying up there before I swung around to the south. I got me a dead aim on the Indian, then I made sure of my angle shot at Malcolm."

"Could you handle both," he said, "if it got tight?"

"No need," Shaffer said. "I met another pilgrim out for a Sunday stroll. He took care of Malcolm."

Shaffer had missed nothing. The sheriff had simply eased in and taken over; and now Kearney wondered how near Malcolm was to the bitter end. Not far, with Montez catching him cold, with Vigil running for his life. The day had served its purpose far better than he hoped; what he had estimated as a month's job, perhaps longer, was now a matter of days.

"Where to?" Shaffer asked.

"The river," he said. "We'll pay that call."

They walked the horses down the canyon into Cedar Springs cove where water bubbled from the rocks and flowed lazily into the river across the long, flattened green grass that was untouched by frost. They dismounted, let the horses drink, and Shaffer saw the light wagon coming off the last switchback across the river.

"There's Flavia," Shaffer said, "and Miguel."

Kearney watched them descend the trail, splash through the shallow water, press wheel tracks against the pale brown sandbar. Flavia wore a gray dress and carried a parasol; her thin face was troubled as he stepped forward and helped her off the wheel to the ground.

"I heard shots," she said.

"A little misunderstanding," Kearney said. "No one hurt . . . is this Miguel?"

"My brother," she said proudly. "Miguel, Señor Kearney."

*"Mucho gusto,"* Miguel Martinez said.

Kearny took the hard, long-fingered hand and met eyes that reminded him entirely of Flavia's, the difference only that Miguel's blazed with his thoughts, spoke openly and concealed no deeper emotions. Miguel was different from Isidro as night was from day, and Miguel spoke his mind bluntly.

"Vigil," he said, "Malcolm?"

"Both," Kearney said. "They learned a lesson today."

"You taught Vigil a lesson!"

"He got careless," Kearney said. "We were evenly matched but he forgot Ed."

"Sonofabitch!" Miguel said. "I knew we should have come sooner—but I talk too much, my sister talks better."

Miguel grabbed Shaffer's arm and pulled him away to the lower end of the sandbar beach. Shaffer said, "—and a mirror!" and Miguel laughed happily and replied with a quick rush of slurred words.

"Please forgive him," she said. "He is always that way."

"Looking for trouble?"

"Oh no," she said. "Making me talk for both."

"Well," he said, "can you?"

"I will try," she said.

She sat on a flat rock above the spring, lowered her parasol, and brushed absently at her hair and sweat-dampened forehead.

"How is your father?" Kearney asked.

"Much better now," she said. "But he feels so bad, for he sees Señor Malcolm without illusion. José stayed in town Saturday. He spoke with friends, and now we know more of you and Señor Malcolm. It is something very bad between you, yes?"

"All the way," Kearney said. "I'd better tell you everything."

He leaned against the rock, busied his fingers with tobacco and paper, and began talking as he had talked to Wintergreen and Shaffer short days ago. When he finished she was sitting ramrod stiff, hands clasped over the parasol handle, watching him intently.

"He is an evil man," she said. "Will you kill him?"

"If it comes to that."

"But must you?" she said sadly. "Must it always end in death?"

"Maybe," Kearney said. "He's on the run now; it depends what he does next, which way he moves."

"I do not approve of killing," she said. "On principle, you understand."

"I know," he said. "Nor do I."

"But we must stand together," she said. "To help you. Because of my father——"

"Your father is safe," Kearney said. "He knows of the land deal, he won't get burned again."

"Yes, but there are other things."

She was coming at last to the painful words. He could picture her talking with Miguel, reviewing the gossip and their own suspicions, wondering, in the evident closeness that existed between them, what Maria would do.

"It is not my father," she said. "Forgive me for bringing our troubles to you, but it is that woman in our house. Please tell me the truth—have you heard the talk?"

"Some," he said. "I take it with a little salt."

"It is true," she said firmly. "We have known for two years. She has been meeting Malcolm. But what could we do? It would kill my father to know. Now you come, you help us greatly, but can you see what might happen?"

"I can see it your way," Kearney said. "You're afraid if I push him too hard, he'll run, but he might tell your father before that. Don't worry, he'll never touch your father."

She shook the parasol in her hands. "I believe you. But what of that woman in our house? She can spoil it all with a word."

98

"Not her," Kearney said. "Would she ruin her own soft bed?"

"Perhaps not," Flavia Martinez said. "But I am ashamed to admit that Malcolm controls her . . . and Teresita is even more dangerous."

"Maybe I can handle that," he said.

"You, señor?"

"I've got to do something about Rachel Perez tonight," Kearney said. "I'll see Teresita."

"You," she said softly. "You can break a curse?"

"I know a little about her business," he said. "I'll put the fear of God in her. That'll hurt Malcolm, eh? That'll push him a little more. You watch your father, watch your stepmother. I'll keep Malcolm busy."

"But call on us," she said, "if you need help."

"I will."

"It was good to speak with you," she said. "Now it is late——"

"Is this all you came for?" Kearney asked bluntly.

She colored suddenly and fumbled with the parasol. It was a trying moment for her and she busied herself with the catch, pushing it up and down the shaft until she regained some measure of her calm. Talking so plainly of her family, she had broken a wall within herself, let down a gate, felt something strange and wonderful enter her heart. John Kearney saw it happen and understood the wild confusion in her eyes, and covered his own confusion by speaking harshly to the team. But words made no difference now; it had passed between them and nothing would be the same until they rode this enigma to the end. And it was so strange, Kearney thought, for she was young and he was beyond youth, yet he had no more experience than she.

"Will I see you again?" he asked.

"If you wish," she said timidly. "I am sure my father will welcome you."

"Your father!" he said. "He'll welcome me, I think Miguel will welcome me. I'd come if only your sheep welcomed me."

He laughed then, saw her mouth lift uncertainly in response, and then they were both smiling when Shaffer and Miguel came from the sandbar. Miguel gave them one sharp, amazed look and could not hide his own grin of absolute pleasure. Then they were shaking hands, saying the good-byes, parting at the spring beside the river.

Teresita McKinley came to the house Sunday afternoon and sat beneath the cottonwood tree in the back yard, watching the big dog prowl restlessly around the wall. Malcolm had left during the night, he had tricked her, but she smiled at the reason. Now she could go home and wait in peace, for Malcolm could never best the Texan in open country. Something would happen out there, Kearney would send him home beaten deeper into the earth. Teresita McKinley went home, sat in her rocking chair, and saw night steal gray across the river and settle black over the town. She leaned forward expectantly when the horse stopped outside, words of tenderness on her tongue as the rider dismounted.

"Carlitos," she called softly.

She saw the tall, dark bulk of the man fill her doorway, and leaped for the shotgun. Kearney's hand caught her wrist, jerked her back, sent her spinning into the rocker. She watched him breech the twelve-gauge, extract the shells, throw the shotgun aside. It clattered on the table and fell against the rawhide trunk. Teresita bent her head to hide the fear that flooded her eyes, but he was too quick. He laughed softly and, where other men spoke foolish bravado, this one held his tongue until she met his gaze.

"I didn't hurt him," Kearney said. "He'll be along."

"Then go!"

"You're coming with me," Kearney said. "To take the curse off a girl named Rachel."

"Ah!" Teresita McKinley said fiercely. "So you do come begging, gringo. I will come with you? I will remove a curse? Now I laugh at *you*, gringo!"

This was a moment of sweet triumph that turned to ashes in her mouth, for he did not react as all gringos should. He did not swear and yell and bluster, threaten her with fist and gun and law. He began talking and the very softness of his words brought a strange fear. It was almost as if he were enjoying chocolate and idle gossip in a sunny room.

"You know where I'm from," Kearney said. "Where you go once in five years to listen and learn, where all you know is nothing but dust compared to those *brujas* of the lower river and the Sierra. They owe me unpaid debts, two are my friends. If you do not take the curse from this girl, I'll put a curse on you that will shrivel you up like a leaf, dry your blood, rot your flesh, turn your bones to powder. You call yourself a great witch because you fool these people, because you use a dog for your trip to the meeting in the Sierra, turn it into a horse and fly? Listen, little witch. Down there they have no need for dogs. They really *fly*. Listen, I'll whisper a name you know, the oldest of the old, who lives in Boquillas, across the river from my home." He was beside her chair, whispering a name she knew in her ear. "If I ask it, she will put a curse on you that cannot come off. You want me to name others, those you live in awe of?"

"No," Teresita McKinley said. *"No!"*

"You believe me now?"

"Yes ... yes."

"Stand up then, little witch."

Teresita McKinley rose from her chair and tried to turn away. She felt his hand touch her braids, pat her right side beneath her dress where she wore the *bolsa* that carried all her *brujerías*, her secrets.

"Good," he said. "All loaded for bear. Where's your *tapalo?*"

She moved blindly to the wall and his hand helped adjust the woolen *rebozo* over her head, slipped downward, felt her arms for the copper rings and bracelets, made sure her top dress button was open.

"All in place," he said. "That's the way I want you."

Then he was leading her from the house, taking her down the road around Malcolm's high wall to Pueblo Road, across the plaza, down Ranchitos Road to the house beside the sheriff's; and the fear of him was like the drawn cords in a dead goat's leg, drawing her against her will through the gate, up the steps into the house. She saw the girl in the darkness of the room, heard the frightened whispers in the kitchen.

"Rachel," Kearney said. "Look up!"

Teresita McKinley saw the girl shrink back, hide her face, try to become a piece with the adobe wall. Then Kearney pushed her forward like a puppet.

"All right, little witch," he said scornfully. "Do your work before I turn you into dust."

The sheriff saw them coming down the road and stepped barefooted off his porch into yard darkness to better trust his eyes. When they passed and went up the steps to his brother's house he was behind them, gun drawn, watching for anything and everything, not excluding ghosts and devils. Standing just outside the doorway, the sheriff saw Teresita McKinley make the motions, say the words that lifted Rachel's face from resignation to unbelieving hope. He stepped aside when Teresita turned and faced Kearney, suddenly old and stooped, and Montez knew he was watching that rarest of sights in all the river country: the end of a *bruja*, the end of all her power over the people.

"Rachel," Kearney said, "are you all right?"

"Yes ... oh yes!"

"Come," Kearney said, and took Teresita's arm. He led her to the porch, a few feet from the sheriff, and turned her down the steps.

"Now we have no quarrel," he said. "But remember, the old one in Boquillas is my friend. I'll speak your name to her, and she does not forget. You hear?"

"I hear."

"Then go home to him," Kearney said.

The sheriff watched her descend the steps, walking like an old woman, scuffing her feet in the dusty road. The sheriff said, "It's me," and fell into step with Kearney as they left the house. "Man, what did you do to her?"

"A dose of her own medicine," Kearney said. "Did you hear it?"

"Yes."

"Now let me thank you for today," he said.

"It was nothing," Montez smiled. "But you missed the fun. When I whistled he jumped like a fox and that gun of his—I thought he'd blow his head off."

"Did you trail him in?"

"Just to Arroyo Hondo," Montez said. "He stopped at the *cantina*. I think he needed a drink, maybe two. He's sweating blood now, and do you realize what you've done to Teresita?"

"Finished her," Kearney said. "It all works together."

"It does," Montez said gravely. "And I understand what you are doing. You have him on the edge."

They stopped outside the sheriff's gate in the dim yellow light dropping through the open door. All was silent, only the wind talked softly down the dusty road.

"How much longer?" Montez asked.

"A week or so," he said.

"Officially I cannot allow violence in town," Montez said, "but unofficially I endorse your action. Still, it would be best for all concerned if you could only arrange it in the country . . ."

"Might not happen that way," Kearney said. "I think he'll run."

"Ah, and you'll let him," Montez smiled. "Surely you will get him then?"

Kearney offered the sheriff a cigar, scratched the match against the gatepost and cupped his hands around the flame.

"Running is best, Montez. If he runs, he leaves everything behind. I might not get him here, but it'll happen sometime, somewhere."

Malcolm turned the mare into the stable and bent to rough up the big dog. One faithful living thing remained with him, he thought, one animal who trusted him without reserve. He had stopped in the Arroyo Hondo *cantina*, drunk off a brandy, ordered drinks for every man present, and knew the full extent of Kearney's presence when all but one drifted away. Only the village drunk staggered to the bar and toasted him in thick-tongued words. Malcolm drank until the fear was dampened, until the shadows were long, before he rode the night trail; and now, entering his house, he found Teresita sitting beside the stove, hands folded in her lap, staring at the lamp.

"Carlitos," she said. "He——"

"Later," Malcolm said thickly.

He carried water to the small room, bathed and shaved, changed into clean clothing, studied his face in the mirror. Returning to the kitchen, sobered by razor and cold water, he sensed the change in her.

"What is the trouble?" he said.

"Nothing—nothing."

"You've seen him?"

"Yes."

Malcolm started the fire, made coffee, brought bread and sausage from the pantry, stood over the stove and sniffed the strong odor. He ate and drank, felt the brandy flame die in his stomach, and glanced covertly at her.

"What did he do to you?"

"He forced me," she said. "He made me remove the curse."

Malcolm led her to a chair in the big room, stood beside her and rubbed her forehead gently. "How could he do that, Teresita?"

He listened as she told of Kearney's knowledge of her kind, of his friends, the great old *brujas* who lived in the Sierra and along the lower river, of the old one in Boquillas who would know her name and never forget.

"And he knows," she said thinly. "I have heard her name, Carlitos. I cannot match her. Now I am ruined here, I must go with you——"

"Go?" Malcolm said. "Are we going, my dear?"

"You cannot stay," she said. "You must go."

Malcolm marshaled the remnants of his life, the remaining valuables he could use: remembrance of a wedding to be held across the river on Thursday, a young man and woman of good families. Don Roberto would attend with all his family . . . that much, Malcolm thought, and the funeral tomorrow for a man who died

Saturday, to be buried in the north cemetery ... his account at the bank, purposely held to a nominal sum ... and Vigil, if the Indian was alive.

"Have you seen Vigil?" he asked.

"No."

"We will wait for him," Malcolm said. "Then we must make our plans."

"To leave?"

"Yes," he said. "And I promise you, when we go, we will go in style."

# Chapter Six

KEARNEY slept until mid-morning, rousing at the boy's knock to enjoy a leisurely breakfast with Jack Wintergreen and Shaffer. Ed had stood guard on the house last night until Malcolm returned, then Vigil, and stayed on to see Vigil and Teresita depart long after midnight; and this morning, spreading like wildfire, was the story of the *bruja's* defeat. Well, he thought, it was all coming to an end. He saw the black hearse and funeral procession moving from Guadalupe Church into Placitas Road, and looked at Wintergreen.

"In the midst of life."

"That's Bob Hanson," Wintergreen said. "Keeled over Saturday."

"Friend of yours?"

"To pass the time of day . . . shame, he wasn't old."

"Accident?"

"Heart," Wintergreen said. "Doc warned him last month, he just kept working. . . . John, what happens now?"

"Sit tight," Kearney said.

"What'll he do next?" Shaffer asked.

"Run."

"But how the hell can you figure that?"

"He's been running all his life," Kearney said. "From wherever he started up to right now. He can't change. He'll run again."

"This is big country," Wintergreen said. "You give him a start, you might not catch him."

"I'll take my chances," Kearney said. "Ed, I want to visit Don Roberto this week."

"Sure," Shaffer said, "but we better go before Thursday. Big wedding across the river, Sanchez boy and Montoya's youngest girl. Don Roberto'll take the whole family down to Montoya's."

My God, he thought, he had been that close to losing it all. He said, "When?"

"Oh, Wednesday morning."

Kearney looked beyond Ed Shaffer, through the front windows into the sunwashed plaza. He saw the sheriff on the courthouse bench, apparently dozing in the shade; and suddenly he had no problem of time and place. If the wedding across the river was common knowledge, which it surely was, then Malcolm knew of it long ago. Once he verified one fact with Flavia and Miguel, he would stake his last dollar on Malcolm's final move. Here then, he thought, or a little later on. It did not matter now.

"Jack," he said. "You can call off the dogs. We'll all leave Wednesday morning."


"Adolfo."

"What is it, Carlos?"

"You want us to keep the watch?"

"Not until tonight," the sheriff said. "Go clean the guns."

The sheriff dozed again, reviewing the morning. Rachel Perez, on his order, had shown herself on the plaza, chattered gaily with friends, arranged to begin her work at the inn tomorrow; and once that news circulated, Teresita McKinley would no longer be a thorn in the sheriff's side. He was smiling to himself when Kearney sat down beside him on the bench.

"Tell me," Kearney said. "Does Malcolm keep a big account at the bank?"

"No," Montez said.

"Can you get word if he cashes out?"

"Five minutes after it happens."

"Thanks," Kearney said. "Well, you want in on the finish?"

"Eh?" Montez said, sitting straight and opening his eyes. "What's this?"

"Be at Don Roberto's Wednesday evening," Kearney said. "You know that big shed south of the house?"

"Yes."

"Meet us there after dark," Kearney said.

"But the family——"

"Will be at Montoya's for the wedding."

"By God!" the sheriff said. "I forgot the wedding." He looked sharply at Kearney, he thought of Don Roberto's distrust in banks, and the final pieces of the puzzle dropped into the frame. Still, it was farfetched. Montez said cautiously, "Can you be sure?"

"Tell me a better way."

"You mean, to leave our town?"

"Yes."

"Now that I think," the sheriff said, "there can be no better way."

"Wednesday night then," Kearney said. "After supper."

Montez watched him cross the plaza, an easy-going man, taking all the time in the world. Oh yes, Montez thought, if only the town had a few more so easy-going. He rose from the bench and walked to his office.

"Carlos," he said. "Go have a beer."

"But I'm just starting on your gun, Adolfo."

"Go on," the sheriff said cheerfully. "This time I better clean it myself."

Vigil sat beneath the cottonwood tree until the services ended and the last mourner's buggy rattled away. He was a hundred yards from the cemetery; the fresh grave was just beyond the fence in the northeast corner. Vigil walked down Pueblo Road and through the front gate into the yard. Malcolm answered his knock, dropped the bar, and led him to the back room where Teresita McKinley favored him with a grunt and continued her work. She was wrapping something in a blanket, folding the ends carefully. Vigil noticed that she was not packing rugs or the Haviland china, and the pictures, ripped from their frames, were crumpled on the floor. But the silver set and the silver picture frames were being wrapped. Vigil approved the selection, and Malcolm, watching him, seemed to read his mind.

"Just the silver," Malcolm said. "No one in this town values china and rugs . . . well, did they finish the services?"

"Yes."

"Where is the grave?"

"Northeast corner," Vigil said. "Close to the road."

"How considerate of them," Malcolm said. "Please clean my rifle, Vigil."

While Vigil busied himself with the Ballard, Malcolm helped Teresita tie the last bundle and make a stack of all. From last night's agony he had finally lifted her to a strange, inverted happiness, as if the prospect of leaving, traveling to another land, was finer in all ways. Once he had explained everything last night she was eager to do her share; and Vigil offered no resistance for he was shamed forever once the story of Sunday reached the pueblo.

"That does it," Malcolm said briskly. "Teresita, one word of caution. Leave your house exactly as you do when taking a trip down the river. Carry no more than you need for such a trip."

"Nothing more, Carlitos."

"Then I suggest you go home and make ready," Malcolm said. "Vigil will stop for you when we leave."

"What time?"

"Quite late," he said. "Be ready."

"Very well, Carlitos."

Malcolm waited until the back door closed before he

sat at the table and motioned Vigil to the other chair. Vigil sat gingerly, unaccustomed to furniture but offering blind obedience to one man.

"We know what must be done tonight," Malcolm said, "but we must talk of another thing before you leave for the afternoon. If you come with me, it must be of your own free will. If you stay, I promise that nothing will happen to you. Think deeply this afternoon, Vigil. Give me your answer tonight."

"I'll go," Vigil said.

"Act in haste," Malcolm said, "repent at leisure."

"No need," Vigil said. "I'll go with you."

"Remember, she goes too."

Vigil walked to the chest and laid the Ballard on the Navaho blanket. He turned as he reached the door, only a moment, and his face lifted in a faint smile.

"You say she goes?"

"Yes."

"She thinks she goes," Vigil said. "I know better."

Vigil was gone then, into the back yard, away from the house. Charles Malcolm found his first smile in two days. He had not fooled Vigil one iota concerning Teresita; but in the play of words and action and feeling, Vigil had betrayed no suspicion regarding himself. Malcolm began pacing the big room, spending the hours, waiting for early evening when he intended to make his final appearance in town. He reviewed it all again, and found no flaw in his plan.

The sheriff sat on the courthouse bench and tasted the sunset feeling of the town. Carlos had gone to watch Malcolm's house from his cousin's yard across Pueblo Road, and Montez did not care how soundly Carlos slept tonight. It made no difference if events followed the ordained pattern: a little peace tonight, tomorrow, all day Wednesday . . . but that night would see the end. Montez spoke to friends, smoked his cigar, sniffed the piñon smoke drifting from the chimneys.

"Ah," he murmured. "Now it does figure!"

For Charles Malcolm came striding into the plaza, tipped his hat to three ladies, paused for a chat with old Tomas Valerio, and followed Tomas into the Beehive Café. Montez followed along, took a front stool, and ordered coffee. Malcolm was further down the counter, eating a bowl of chili, while Tomas talked seriously, waving both hands to emphasize a point. Montez strained his ears and heard Tomas explain that he held Urbino's note which was due next month and if he, Valerio, was not forced to leave for Las Cruces and needed cash, he would not sell the note at forty per cent discount. Malcolm shook his head and said, "Sorry, Tomas. Not now." And that was the first time in six years, so far as Montez knew, that Malcolm had turned down an easy profit. He slipped outside and returned to the courthouse bench, thoroughly convinced at last. Such a little thing, he thought, but it proved Kearney's judgment beyond all doubt.

And what was he doing, the duly elected sheriff of Taos County, about to abet violence? Planning to cross the river, help a virtual stranger kill a respected member of their community. Such action surely proved that he was not only derelict in his duty but downright murderous to boot. To help a stranger—and a Texan at that—do violence to a townsman. Well, that was how it might look in a courtroom. But the sheriff had lived too long in his own valley world to place much emphasis on courts. A man learned to follow his eyes and ears in this country, to judge men and stick by that judgment. And there were crimes never listed in a court docket: robbing innocents, playing benevolent father with one hand and poking the devil's trident with the other. Montez knew nearly everything tonight and, with that shrewd intuition, guessed the balance. If he were forced to stand before the final Judge and defend his action he would say of Malcolm, "The man deserves to die!" For, like Kearney, the sheriff possessed deep understanding of those tortures which pursued a man and made his living far more agony than death. It would be interesting, come Wednesday night, to see which method Kearney chose: continued torture of the mind, or death, final and absolute. That was only natural; the dark old savage Spanish blood was still heavy in his veins.

Early evening was such a peaceful time in the town. Supper was over, fires were dying in the stoves and ovens. Sunset was fading across the river, night wind off the Cristos swept down from the north, from Colorado through San Luis Valley, over Wheeler Peak and along Twining Canyon into the Hondo, through all the narrow, nameless canyons bending ever into the river; dancing through the turning aspens at timberline, and red willows along the creeks, rippling the water in the beaver dams. People were talking on the porches, in the back yards, on the shadowed plaza benches; the goats, milked, wandered again to the soft, wet *vega* bottoms. Wind moved gently beneath the white clouds and deep blue sky, dogs barked and coyotes answered from the loma, thin and sharp and lonesome in the falling night. One man could come and cause a tiny ripple across the centuries of the town, the valley, but one man could never change and conquer. One man made a tiny ripple, for a little while, and then he went away.

They slipped from the back gate, carrying the shovel and folded stretcher, and moved along the path that wound past Teresita's house toward the pueblo. They left the path east of the cemetery and crept across Pueblo Road into the high, dusty weeds that lined the cemetery fence. Charles Malcolm drew his bulldog .38 and knelt beside the fence. Vigil rolled beneath the bottom strand and ran to the grave, laid the wreaths aside, and began digging into the unpacked earth.

"Quiet," Malcolm whispered. "Watch the spade!"

"*Bueno.*"

Vigil worked swiftly, lifted out his load and placed it on the stretcher, refilled the grave, patted down the earth, set the wreaths in place. Vigil pushed the loaded stretcher under the fence, Malcolm took the rear handles, and Vigil led the way. Walking slowly, following the deepest shadows, they circled eastward to the path and returned unseen through the back gate. The dog growled uncertainly when they lowered the stretcher beside the table in the big room. Vigil moved over against the wall and made a secret, cabalistic sign with one hand.

"Saddle the horses," Malcolm said. "Tie the packages on."

Vigil gathered the packages and ran from the house. Malcolm went to the kitchen, poured half a glass of whisky and downed it neat, then turned and nerved himself for the dismal task. But first he went to his small bedroom where the iron-strapped box was open beside the hole, gave it one last kick for better effect, and packed the leather draw purses and flat oilcloth packages in his saddlebags. He carried the bags and his Ballard to the kitchen, laid them on the table, and faced the wall beside the stove where all the kitchen tools hung neatly. "Poor Yorick," he said wryly. "You know not whom you represent."

And then he swallowed the thickness in his throat and began the work that took fifteen terrible minutes. He was in the kitchen with another glass, white-faced but composed, when Vigil returned.

"You done?" Vigil asked.

"Finished," Malcolm said. "Get Teresita, meet me in the field west of her house."

"*Bueno.*"

Then he was alone, and it was time to go. He had to leave the dog, and that in many ways was worst of all. Malcolm knelt, took the rough ears between his hands, and spoke softly in words that made no sense but lifted a growl of love from the big dog's throat. He stood then, lifted the Ballard and the saddlebags, and looked at the house he had built to his own shape and image, the only house he had owned in all his years of running, of searching, of believing in the dream that never quite came true. But the house was only wood and adobe, there were other lands and houses, there were finer dreams ahead.

"*Oso,*" he said softly. "Good-bye."

Kearney watched the plaza Tuesday but Malcolm did not appear; Tuesday night wore on, he slept, to rise at four o'clock with Shaffer and Wintergreen, saddle the horses, and take the west road. One man saw them go. Montez had sat through the night on his porch, wrapped in a thick Navaho blanket, a Two Gray Hills blanket taken from a horse thief five years ago. He saw them pass, finished his beer, and went to bed; and north of the plaza in his cousin's front yard, Carlos Ramos slept on, just as he had slept the previous night. It did not matter now; his easy dollars were gone.

Wednesday morning was a time of excited preparation in every house across the river. Don Roberto gave orders right and left, organizing his own caravan, thinking happily of the wedding celebration. He was so busy he did not see Ed Shaffer enter the ranch yard, signal his daughter, and meet her behind the big shed. If he noticed his daughter at all that morning it was with regret that she was not preparing for her own wedding, that he was not awaiting the arrival of the groom's family with their wagonload of food, the leather trunks carrying the bride's trousseau and wedding gown, and all the gifts. Don Roberto shouted hoarsely, stomped about his house, while Ed Shaffer brought Kearney's message.

"You know for sure where your father keeps his money?" Shaffer asked.

"In the office," Flavia said. "Under the floor."

"All right," Shaffer said. "You and Miguel get away from Montoya's, get back here and move that box. Can you do it right after sunset?"

"Yes," she said calmly. "And then?"

"We'll be here," Shaffer said. "You move the box and come to this shed."

"Does he truly think Malcolm will come tonight?"

"You know him," Shaffer said. "He can't seem to guess wrong about Malcolm—— Ho, your father's about ready."

"Adios," she said. "Tonight, then."

Don Roberto did not miss Flavia in the turmoil of loading everyone in the buggies. His wife swept from the house and took her place in the new buggy, ignoring the others as she clasped her hands and stared sullenly at the horses. Isidro counted his children, signaled to his father, and they were off. Don Roberto whistled as he rode, forgetting his troubles, leading his family into Montoya's yard with a shout. By suppertime he was enjoying himself so fully that he did not miss Flavia and Miguel.

They waited until full dark before riding off the slope to the shed. Wintergreen tied the horses inside and they waited against the wall; and the sheriff arrived ten minutes later, greeted them softly, and led his black horse inside. When Montez joined them, carrying rifle and rope, Kearney spoke.

"See anybody coming in?"

"No one," Montez said. "If they are here, it would be north above the spring, I think. Have you informed the family?"

"Flavia and Miguel."

"Not Don Roberto?"

"No," he said curtly. "Ed, take a look."

Shaffer walked to the west corner and immediately whispered, "*¿Quién es?*" and returned with Flavia and Miguel. Kearney shook hands with Miguel, found her hand and felt it tighten in his.

"Is it moved?" he asked.

"Yes," Miguel said. "In the kitchen under the wood. We put a log in its place."

"Who else is in the house?"

"No one," Flavia said. "Only Lupe, but she is eighty-two and asleep and deaf also. Give the orders, Señor Kearney. Where do we wait?"

"You here," he said. "Miguel, you and Ed on the east side facing the front door. Jack, you here at the corner. Sheriff, will you go behind the house?"

"*Bueno.*"

"Miguel," Kearney said, "will you please have a lantern with you?"

"There's one here in the shed," Miguel said.

"Good . . . now, if they come, wait until they enter the house. Your father's office has no window on the east side, eh?"

"No window."

"Once they are inside," Kearney said, "run to the front door, place the lantern on the ground about ten steps out from the doorway. Light it and get back to your position."

"Ah," Miguel said. "And when they dig up the log and start to run—very good, Kearney!"

"And you," Flavia said, "where will you be?"

"In the house," he said.

"No!"

"Yes," Kearney said. "Now listen—if they come, try not to hurt the woman, don't go for Vigil unless he forces you."

"And Malcolm?" she asked.

He said, "Why do you think I'm here?" and walked from the shed, around the corner, across the silent yard to the house. Remembering his only visit, the office door was some ten paces down the front hall, across from the short side hall leading to the kitchen. Kearney entered the office, scratched a match and looked for the white kidskin rug beside the table. He lifted one corner, felt the earth, and nodded approval of Miguel's job. He went from the office through the side hall into the kitchen, found a three-legged stool, and set it against the wall beside the hallway. He checked his Colt, hammer and trigger, dropped the sixth cartridge through the loading gate into the empty chamber; and sat wide-legged on the stool in the aromatic darkness of the kitchen. Minutes later he heard a scuffing sound in the rear and whirled, Colt up, as she called softly, "Señor Kearney?" and came forward to place another stool and sit beside him in the darkness.

"This is no place for you," he said.

"This is my house," she said quietly.

He could offer no argument to that simple speech; it typified her completely, the way he had seen her from the beginning. He had known a few like her along the lower river, only a few, for they were rare and wonderful in their quiet, self-effacing way. Those he had known were older, women with grown children and grandchildren, going about the operation of great houses and haciendas with no more fuss than baking a cake, having in them all the dignity and the fineness a man might hope for and never touch. This was her home; therefore she must be here.

"Will he come?" she asked.

"I'm betting on it."

"But this far?" she said. "I think I know that man. His kind would send another—send Vigil."

"Possible."

"Then you will miss him, for Vigil will surely give the alarm."

"No matter," Kearney said. "Look, if you won't be sensible, at least get out of the hallway."

"Oh . . . you are right."

She moved her stool across the hallway to the other wall and settled there quiet as a mouse. Kearney rolled a cigaret and tasted the unlit tobacco, yearning as always for the forbidden smoke.

"Señor Kearney?"

"Yes."

"Are you always right?" she said timidly. "In everything you do?"

"Me?" he said. "Lord no."

"I have been wrong so many times," she said. "I wish I could think as you, decide quickly and firmly."

"About what?" he asked.

"So many things."

"No," he said bluntly, "that's not what you mean, Flavia. Let's settle this now. Did you feel anything Sunday? Tell me if you did . . . don't lie. I can't spout the pretty words, I can just say what I feel. What did you feel Sunday?"

"I do not know," she said.

"But you felt something?"

"Yes," she said softly. "But please, this is not proper . . ."

"Why not?" he said. "It's you and me, nobody else."

"You should speak to my father," she said. "You do not live here, you are going away. . . . Please, this is not right."

"You're healthy," he said. "You can travel, live in another place."

"But, señor," she said, so softly he strained to hear the words, "you do not know me."

"All I need to," he said. "Don't you know me?"

"No," she said. "Yes . . . I . . ."

"Well, by God," Kearney said, "you see, we both know. Why should it take six months, a year? Calling on Sunday, sitting in the *sala,* saying all those stupid, foolish words? Why can't it happen this way? I've got no patience with any of it, with women like that—a dime a dozen. All I do is feel, and I feel it."

"But I am old," she said. "I am twenty-four. That is so old."

"Old?" Kearney said. "You and I, we'll never be old and you know it. . . . But you want me to see your father, eh? All right, I'll sit on his knee, sing to him, but it won't make any difference, will it . . . will it?"

"No," she said. "No, it will not. I——"

"Hush!" he whispered.

Monday had been a miserable night in the upper range. Malcolm chose a campsite on the ridge above his ranch and sat shivering in his blanket as he thought of the warmth below, the bed and fire and hot coffee. They moved down the Red next morning, lay quiet during the day, and crossed the Rio that night at Cedar Springs; then it was easy to circle north and west into the jumbled rimrock ten miles above Don Roberto's. Vigil started a fire and slipped away to mount guard; and Teresita sat shivering beside that tiny fire. He sat close to her for mutual warmth and thought of the big house below, and the woman there he would not see again, and some of his anger touched her ever-receptive mind. He had brought a bottle and, within the hour, had drunk too deeply to control his emotions. He saw her eyes in the dying firelight as she turned to him, and the effort of refusal was too much then. When it was over and she lay beside him, stretching like a cat, whispering softly in his ear, he allowed it all with indifference. Only the chance that Vigil might return at any moment spared him the balance of the night. She was sleeping across the fire when Vigil reported all clear to the south; and then it was a matter of passing the night, and the day, until now, long after dark, they stood beside their horses a mile above the ranch yard. Malcolm motioned them together, draped a blanket over their heads, lit a match and scratched an outline of the front hall and office, showing the location of the box beneath the kidskin rug.

"It will not be too heavy," Malcolm said. "If you cannot break the lock, bring the box. Is it all clear, Vigil?"

"*Bueno.*"

"Teresita will hold the horses," Malcolm said. "I will follow you in five minutes, take a position just above the house."

"No," Vigil said, "no closer. Stay here."

"You think it best?" he said.

"Nobody home," Vigil said. "I watched today. Everybody went to Montoya's. Better just one man."

Vigil grunted and slipped away into the night. Charles Malcolm turned to his mare and rubbed his damp palms against the smooth hair, trembling now that his last gambit had played as hoped: that Vigil was too proud to accept help in so easy a task, that he must redeem himself for all the mistakes of the past. Teresita moved over and pressed against his arm. She had grown more possessive during the day; her look and her speech spoke a language even Vigil understood. But Vigil knew, and he knew, that all her dreams of the future were as dust. And now she began talking of Chihuahua, of the life they would have in the city, or even further to the south.

"Where will we cross, Carlitos?" she said. "El Paso . . . the Presidio. Remember, I heard that Kearney has friends watching in those places."

"A small matter," Malcolm said carelessly. "That means nothing . . . it depends on the fighting."

"Yes, Villa is in Juarez," she said thoughtfully. "But he would not harm us, Carlitos."

"Villa would shoot his grandmother," Malcolm said flatly. "I want no truck with him, my dear."

"Then further down the river, eh?"

"We shall see," he said.

"Ah," she said suddenly. "I have thought of something wonderful. Let us cross at Boquillas. Where *he* lives, Carlitos. Would that not be a great trick?"

"We will see," Malcolm said curtly. "Never anticipate."

"Very well. . . . But how will we go from here?"

He saw no reason to lie about that. He reviewed the planned route west into the heavy timber, south past Ojo Caliente, Santa Fe, Albuquerque, then back on the river road below Socorro and on through Las Cruces to the border.

"I have a friend in Las Cruces," Teresita said. "We can trust her, Carlitos."

"We trust no one," he said.

"True, we carry much of value . . . what do you think Don Roberto has in his box?"

Charles Malcolm had considered that question for two years. He estimated at least fifty thousand in coin and paper; depending on the weight, it might prove wise to cache the coin and carry only paper. But that could be settled when Vigil returned.

"A few thousand," he said. "Well worth our time."

"Carlitos," she said. "We have much time now."

"Please," Malcolm said wearily. "This is the time to rest. Sit down. Vigil will be gone at least an hour."

Vigil came off the last slope through the trees and sniffed the silence, listened to the night below. He carried his rifle and the small crowbar Malcolm had provided. He heard no sound as he crossed the yard and pushed the front door inward; he slipped inside, walked ten steps, and felt the office door on his left. Inside at once, the door closed behind him, Vigil dropped to his knees. He found the rug beside the table, pushed it aside, and tested the earth. It was loose; this was the spot. He drew the candle from his shirt, scratched a match, and set the candle beside the table leg. Then he dug with crowbar and fingers, six inches, a foot, and struck solidness; and knew, even as he brushed the dirt away, that he touched a log, not an iron-strapped strongbox. In that moment Vigil crouched breathless above the hole; then he pinched the candle flame, dropped the crowbar, and leaped to his feet. He opened the door and paused, unwilling to retreat through a strange house, yet knowing what waited outside the front door. It was all over for him, he knew that, and he knew that Malcolm had tricked him in the end. He could drop the rifle and call to whoever watched around this house; and nothing very bad would happen; but all that was bad had happened within him by now. Vigil walked to the door, swung it open, and there on the ground before the doorway was a lighted lantern. He was bathed in that yellow glow and from the darkness beyond he heard Ed Shaffer call, "Drop it, Vigil!"

Kearney came off the stool when the front door opened and sent a breath of cold air coursing through the house. He heard the man advance, enter the office, close the door. He crossed over in one step, pushed Flavia away from the corner, and whispered in her ear, "Stay here!" and stood, shielding her, looking up the short hallway into darkness.

When the office door opened he could almost smell the man's anger—not fear, for the man made no foolish move—and then the front door swung back and Shaffer called, "Drop it, Vigil!" and he ran up the short hall, rounded the corner, and saw the Indian. Vigil faced the outer darkness, poised for flight, then exploded violently, firing two shots over the lantern toward Shaffer's voice, levering his rifle so swiftly the sounds blurred, leaping directly for the lantern, covering ten steps in two jumps and bringing one foot forward in a vicious arc to blot out the treacherous light; and the shot caught him in mid-stride, spun him around the lantern in a grotesque dance of shadow and yellow light, crashed him to the earth as his rifle dropped and his right foot came to rest against the metal lantern base.

"John!" Shaffer called.

"Swing north," he answered.

He bumped Flavia as he raced for the kitchen, swung her aside, rushed between the tables and chairs, found the other door beside the woodbox, and ran into the night. Montez called from above the spring, "Climb the slope!" and they were all moving in a rough line, himself and Montez on the west, Jack closing up the middle, Shaffer and Miguel on the east. They pushed to the very top of the ridge where Montez halted them and expressed his opinion: Malcolm was not here, Vigil had come alone.

"Horses," Kearney said. "Jack . . . Ed."

When they reached the yard, Flavia was standing beside the lantern, watching Vigil. Miguel knelt down for a moment and shook his head.

"He's done."

"Was it you?" Montez asked.

"Yes," Miguel said. "There was no choice, Sheriff."

"I know," Montez said sadly. "But perhaps it is best for him. Often, the way we live, the way he lived, a man does not have a choice."

Then Ed and Jack had the horses, the others ran to mount, and Kearney drew her away from the lantern, into the doorway, holding her arms, seeing her face in the yellow light for the first time that night.

"You're all right?"

"Yes," she said calmly.

"Wait inside," he said. "Promise?"

"Very well," she said. "And if you do not come back tonight?"

"All of you must come to town tomorrow," he said. "I will see you then."

He ran to his horse and followed them up the slope to the north; but they had only cleared the first ridge when Montez said, "No chance tonight . . . if he is really here."

"I'll go on," Kearney said.

"Believe me," Montez said. "If we had one chance—but out here, no."

"No matter," Kearney said.

"Man, you take it coolly."

"Take what?"

"Missing him," Montez said. "You realize you may

never have another chance? Too bad, too bad . . . all this for nothing."

"Nothing?" Kearney said. "He's lost it all and himself to boot. That's what I came for."

"But him . . . to keep on living!"

"A little while maybe," Kearney said. "Let him enjoy it now."

The shot sound came faint but clear on the night. Two shots, then another, and then silence. Malcolm pushed Teresita to the horses, helped her mount, led the way north and west. She said, "Vigil?" but he slashed her horse with his quirt and took her up the ridge in the darkness. Well, he thought, and had he really expected to walk in freely and scoop up Don Roberto's strongbox? Kearney had guessed it all, to the very end, and in doing so had outguessed himself. For no man, no troop of men, could search him out tonight in this land.

Malcolm began the long ride away from everything he had gained, with only the woman and the saddlebags to show his profit. He carried twenty thousand in the saddlebags, and the woman did not count. Lost, he thought, lost was the house, the ranch, the mine, the bank account, the woman he wanted; and all he had was life. And then he chuckled, for what else did a man need? He rode through the night, to the west and south around Tres Piedras, riding and resting, riding into pale dawn, stopping for water, riding into the morning that grew bright with sunshine that ate the shadows from their faces.

They skirted Ojo Caliente that day and moved slowly along the base of the mountains until Malcolm found the canyon leading downward to the river just below San Ildefonso. He called the first halt in a mass of rocks, tied the horses, helped her to a seep spring where she drank and rubbed her legs and sighed with the pain. He had no wish to prolong the game; nor did he want a final scene replete with words and gestures. She had debased him two nights ago and, even now, collecting sticks for the supper fire, he could feel her restored confidence, sense the growing strength of her newly-discovered domination. Give her a week and she would own him, body and soul.

He made a final show of watching their back trail while she laid the fire star-fashion and fumbled in her levis for a match. He drew the .38 and shot her once behind the ear, caught her as she fell, and carried her higher into the rocks. He built up a cairn, scattered the fire sticks, untied the horses, and led hers as he picked his way down the canyon toward the river. Within ten days he would forget all this, forget as easily as he had in the past, go forward to something fresh and new. And today, he thought, they should enter his house and find him dead, and what would Kearney say?

There was great excitement in town on Thursday afternoon. Don Roberto and his family arrived; the sheriff handled the formalities in a dignified way that did nothing to harm Don Roberto and helped a great deal toward silencing the talk concerning his wife. Kearney sat in the dining room with Flavia Martinez, drinking endless cups of black coffee, talking more freely now, waiting for her father. He had given up the search at midnight, cut across country to Cedar Springs, and caught the others on the Hondo road; and now he waited for the final proof: was Malcolm home, or was the house deserted? He looked through the windows and saw Ed Shaffer running across the plaza, others following, entering the dining room and charging his table. Montez was very white, and spoke with difficulty.

"We went to Malcolm's," Montez said. "Just now."

"He wasn't there, eh?"

"Yes," Montez said. "He is there."

He said, "What is it?" and saw their faces and understood the sheriff's reluctance before a woman.

"Tell it, man," Flavia said. "You think I'm a lily?"

"Listen," Montez said thickly.

He told it all, the beginning of a legend in the valley, a story that went on and on, unsettled through the years. They had broken the door, entered the house, and found the body in the back room. The big dog was in the kitchen, like a fighting bull in a ring corner, defying them all. Carlos had run around and opened the kitchen door, the big dog leaped outside, slashed at Carlos, ran through the back gate and past Teresita's house toward the pueblo. A deputy on guard became excited and shot the dog; but that was forgotten as they all stood in the room, looking down on the body and becoming sick. They could not tell who it was from the face, but it was Malcolm in size and shape, it wore Malcolm's fine clothing. The silver was gone, the pictures ripped from those frames, the strongbox was in the bedroom, looted. Teresita's house was empty, Vigil was dead; and when they began putting all the pieces together, who else knew where Malcolm kept his money, who else could enter his house freely?

"So it is over," Montez said. "Not as you hoped, perhaps, but done."

"You want to go over?" Shaffer asked.

"No," he said. "If you don't need me."

"No one can do a thing," Montez said gently. "Therefore, if you will excuse me——"

Montez rushed away to take charge of the legalities. Kearney sat unmoving beside Flavia and looked at Shaffer, smiled faintly at Jack Wintergreen.

"You both saw it?" he asked.

"We were inside first," Wintergreen said.

"What do you think?" he said.

"What the town'll think, you mean," Wintergreen said, "or what we figure, knowing what we do?"

"What you think," he said.

"I'd never admit this in public," Wintergreen said, "but I don't think that dead man is Malcolm."

"Who then?"

"Listen," Wintergreen said softly. "Somebody died Saturday, was buried Monday. They were the same age, of a size and shape. But we don't dare speak up now, do we?"

"By God!" Shaffer said, "I'd hate to think——"

"Don't think," Kearney said. "But do a few things for me, get Montez to help. I'll turn over my papers to you.

All the names of the people he hurt and robbed. Let Montez push through the legal work, declare him dead. There'll be no relatives claiming his estate. Split it between these folks who sent me, between the children here. You can do it, legal or not."

"And you?" Flavia said.

"I'm long overdue back home," Kearney said. "I'll be leaving soon as possible."

She ignored them and took his arm. "And my father?"

"Ed, Jack," Kearney said, "we'll get together tonight, eh? I've got some business right here."

He watched their faces lift in the smiles that meant so much; then they were scraping their boots, promising to be handy in any emergency, grinning openly at Flavia, leaving them alone. She still held his arm, and he took her hand and said, "I've got to leave no later than tomorrow afternoon. Do we see your father now?"

"He will be alone," she said, "with that woman——"

"That's his woman," Kearney said. "And his life. I told you that while we sat here and drank coffee and made up our minds an hour ago . . . or have you changed your mind?"

"No," she said suddenly. "No, but it is so swift. . . . Yes, one thing."

"One thing?" Kearney said impatiently. "I thought you were the one who was saying never mind the talk a while ago."

"I was," she said. "I was. But the other, that business of dividing his estate. What if that is done, and then he returns?"

"Oh, that?" Kearney said quietly. "Let it die. . . . He won't be back."

# Chapter Seven

CHARLES Malcolm followed his guide down Screwbean Creek, through the last dry wash, along the cutbank trail to the river. The Big Bend in November was bright and hot and dry, wild and lonely and forgotten at the entrance to Boquillas Canyon where the Rio Grande slipped silently between sheer walls, into perpetual shadow, and began the last secret journey northward before turning southeast for the final time and coursing on to the gulf. Across the river on the low bluff, the village of Boquillas lay brown against the brown earth, old adobe houses, some roofed with battered tin; old smuggler's crossing, the end of the world for Mexico and the United States. And running southward two hundred empty miles from Boquillas, a trail led through Ocampo and thence toward the capital.

He had left the eastbound passenger train at Marathon yesterday morning, hired a guide and bought a horse within the hour, and had ridden the hundred miles south since then. He had especially enjoyed last night's camp at Glenn Springs, inquiring for an old friend named John Kearney, learning that Kearney's ranch paralleled his trail all the way to the river. That was poetic justice, riding in the very shadow of Kearney's home; it made the final mile much sweeter, knowing that Kearney was chasing ghosts in New Mexico.

Charles Malcolm paid his guide the balance of the price, added a bonus, and urged his horse into the water. He would hire native guides in Boquillas; by nightfall he would be deep in a wild, lonely land. He splashed through the north channel, the middle stream sandbar, then the south channel, and rode his horse up the gentle bank toward the green willows. He smiled with the growing triumph he had nurtured for ten long days. The past was fading, forgotten, the future lay ahead, fresh and bright, the dream that would never end. He looked up at the green willows and heard the words.

"Good morning, Malcolm!"